BACK TO
LIFE

SERENDIPITY BOOK ONE

BACK TO
LIFE

KT BOND

4 Horsemen
Publications, Inc.

Back to Life
Serendipity Series Book 1
Copyright © 2021 KT Bond. All rights reserved.

4 Horsemen
Publications, Inc.

4 Horsemen Publications, Inc.
1497 Main St. Suite 169
Dunedin, FL 34698
4horsemenpublications.com
info@4horsemenpublications.com

Cover by *Ron Perry Graphic Design, rperrydesign.com*
Typesetting by Autumn Skye
Editor CI Stearn

Library of Congress Control Number: 2021948919

Print ISBN: 978-1-64450-421-5
Ebook ISBN: 978-1-64450-420-8
Audio ISBN: 978-1-64450-419-2

DEDICATION

For Maurits ... you are, and have been since we first met, one of a very select group of people whom I am thrilled to call my dear friend. And you have been more than just my friend. We were English teachers together, you in your Dutch town, me in my American city, sharing our teaching and our writing lives. You have been a blessing and an inspiration to me. Thank you for all you do every day to show me that you believe in me and support me in all my endeavors. This first novel is for you, *liefje*, with my fondest thoughts.

And for Lloyd ... my love always. Sleep in peace, big brother, until we meet again "somewhere out there."

ACKNOWLEDGMENTS

This first novel might not have been possible if a friend hadn't introduced me to Literotica.com, a site where I could post my erotic romances and still keep my own copyright. That site has opened doors for me that would have remained closed had I not begun there when I did. So, Bill, thank you for showing me the way.

My friend Maurits is an actual Dutchman, and he ensured that the cultural and other Dutch references I made were accurate. He even taught me the few Dutch phrases I didn't already know, the most important one being that for "I love you." I loved doing research with such an authentic source. You are as wonderful a cultural resource as you are a friend, M. *Heel erg bedankt, mijn vriend.* Thank you very much.

My beta readers spoke the truth to me about what needed adjusting, developing, or trashing. Ruby, as a published author in your own right, you're an inspiration to me, young lady. I'm happy that we're able to help each other in this way. You've read for me before, and I've always found your insights helpful. It's always a delight to work with you.

Linda, you're my sister from another mister … or whatever the right thing is to say about a sister soulmate whom I met five years ago at Yale University's Writer's Conference. It can't be a coincidence that we were fellow educators, as well as sharing all the other points of similarity that have bound us to each other since that wonderful summer week, including now being writing partners. Thank you, dear one, for your faith in me.

Then, much gratitude goes to my cover designer, who was my friend first. Ron, your creativity and professionalism are as stellar as your friendship. I appreciate you more than I can say, and I am looking forward to an epic publishing journey with you in my corner. Thank you, my friend.

Finally, to all those of you who have believed in me, have encouraged me, and have read my stories and wondered what I was waiting for to begin my journey, my warmest affection and gratitude. I wouldn't be here now, feeling this buoyed up, this ready to go, were it not for you. And whatever happens with this first novel, I'm excited and thrilled to be able to do it with you all at my back.

And yes, Stephie, Mila and Bas are coming. :)

TABLE OF CONTENTS

CHAPTER 1

I t had been a long day, and Karen Mullings was too tired to care much about where she ate. She just needed dinner and her bed. She walked into the hotel's restaurant and waited to be seated. The table for two was in the quietest corner, which suited her just fine. Although she had happily embarked on this solo European tour, and though she had enjoyed every city she had stayed in, she still preferred to hide away at dinnertime. It was a little sad that a grown woman would be alone for dinner every day, though she had no pressing need of a companion. After three aborted marriage attempts to men with whom she had not been in sync, she was happy to be alone. However, she did feel her aloneness most sharply in the evenings, which was why she more often than not called room service for dinner.

Today, however, she knew if she went up to her room, she would fall asleep without eating, and when she woke, both the restaurant and room service would be unavailable. So, she ordered the house special for the evening and a glass of red wine, and stretched her feet out under the table, letting the peace and quiet soak into her bones. After swallowing almost the whole glass of water thoughtfully provided for her, she hurried to the ladies' room.

On the way out, she bumped into someone going in the opposite direction, almost falling over. Only his quick hands and steady feet kept her on her own. The arm around her, dangerously close to her bottom, was hard and muscled, his grip strong and sure at her waist. The man's shoulders were wide, and he was taller than she was by a good six inches. His eyes were the prettiest blue she had ever seen, reminding her of the Caribbean Sea on a hot summer day.

"I ... I'm so sorry!" she exclaimed, pulling herself up to her full height and looking up at the stranger.

His full lips smiled at her, and his dimpled cheeks surprised her. "That's okay. I'm glad to help. Are you all right now?"

He withdrew his hand from her back. They were hard, manly hands, long-fingered and heavily veined. She felt the loss immediately. It made no sense to feel that way, and it disturbed her.

"Yes, I'm fine. Thank you!"

She smiled in her turn and excused herself, hurrying back to her table. The food, when it was served, was hot, filling, and delicious as usual. She was glad of something to take her mind off the still unsettling encounter with the handsome, blue-eyed man outside the restroom. She savored a second glass of wine in lieu of dessert, then went to pay her bill. As she turned toward the elevators, her mystery encounter rounded the corner and their eyes met for the second time. Something like an electric charge shot up her arms and settled in her chest. He flashed those shocking dimples again, acknowledging her with a nod before walking out through the wide glass doors with his companions, two women and another man. She went up to her room in a daze.

After a hot shower, during which she tried to escape the thoughts of the dark-haired stranger with the sexy mouth and husky voice, she rubbed lotion into her skin and crawled into bed. She had enjoyed her day out and about in Amsterdam but was now thoroughly exhausted and hoped she would sleep undisturbed. Tomorrow, she would be visiting the Oude Kerk and the Dam Plein, and she knew she would need reserves of energy for the long walking and standing about.

Sometime during the night she awoke, shaking and wet. Then the dream came crashing in on her waking mind. She had been dreaming about the smiling stranger and the way his large man's hands had brought her such pleasure while his dimples beamed at her. She rushed from the bed to the bathroom to relieve herself, hoping she could escape from the eroticism of it. Her relationships had all failed, even when she had thought she loved the men involved. Her heart had been bruised one too many times, so she was very wary of men and mistrusted her feelings for them on principle. To dream about a perfect stranger as she had done was unprecedented and extremely unsettling, even though she was very aware of her allure. When she did trust men, though, she was very willing to share the depth and breadth of her passion with them. She just needed a break, a chance to catch herself before she tried again. She took a glass of water with her back to bed and flipped through the TV channels until she found some mindless comedy to occupy her so that she grew drowsy again and fell back on her pillows.

Almost two hours away in Leeuwarden, Peter van der Meulen sipped a second glass of brandy and stared into the fireplace. He had not been able to get the woman in the restaurant out of his mind. That brief contact had fired his imagination and his desires like nothing else had in years, not since the earliest days with Alijd, who had died four years before after twenty years of marriage. The woman was everything Alijd had not been. She had been wearing jeans and a loose shirt with a scoop neckline, so Peter got a good up-close view of her chest. She looked to be about late thirties with beautiful brown eyes, a bright ravishing smile, nice long legs, and delicious-looking breasts. She was a little plump, which was exactly the way Peter liked a woman to be.

He wondered who she was, how she came to be in Amsterdam, and why she was alone. She was the most alluring woman he had seen in years, and he found himself wanting to meet her again, to get to know her, perhaps even become friends. It was unexpected, this interest in a stranger. Peter was nothing if not conservative in public, and in fact, his few friends often had to encourage him to loosen up and enjoy himself. But this woman made him feel as though he were completely out of all control with the way he had been feeling since he got back home. Perhaps, for his peace of mind, he needed to forget her and get on with the business of his life. He had some tests to mark—the thought made him groan—and then he had to prepare for his next week's classes. Monday was fast approaching.

He drained the glass and took it to the sink where he rinsed it and turned it over to dry before going into his office to begin the work that never stopped. He taught English in a nearby secondary school, and his pupils ranged in ability from the apparently terminally lazy to the impossibly brilliant, with a fair number of average Joes in between. He sighed as he picked up his pencil and began to mark the batch of tests he had stopped halfway through. He worked through the rest of that one and the next one before giving up in favor of some jazz and a book. He could wait to tackle the last two tomorrow during his non-teaching periods.

His job was a demanding one, despite some people's perception that teaching was easy. Given that he was obliged by law to work until he was almost sixty-seven, he found he needed the holidays he took as often as he could to refresh him and help him stay the course. The visit to Amsterdam had been one such break away from the routine of his life, and he had enjoyed it to the max. His chance encounter occupied his thoughts greatly over the course of the next two months, during which he had no opportunity to do more than visit the occasional local museum or go out to dinner with a friend.

Despite his first intentions to forget her, he kept that chance encounter fresh in his memory, though he couldn't say why he did so. He refreshed the vision of her in his mind often during his workdays which were of uniform length but not of equal challenge. On those days when he had long, unscripted time to himself, he chose to conjure her face as he marked papers or planned lessons. She became a welcome respite from the inanity of some of his colleagues' chatter and a kind of beacon for the times when he felt lonely. He knew it was a fanciful and probably foolish way to occupy his mind, but there was no harm in it to anyone, and if it gave him a reason to smile, why should he regret it?

Two months later, on the annual school trip that brought him to London this year, Peter found himself standing in the British Museum, alone for the time being. His colleagues had gone off with the students they had brought with them, and he was making his way back to them from a restroom stop when he saw his mystery woman again. The sight of her brought him up short. She was transfixed by the work of art she stood before, her gaze rapt, and no doubt, by the earbuds in her ears, she was listening to a description of the piece she was looking at. She was in jeans snuggling up to her round bottom and hugging her long legs. Her top was loose, but he could clearly tell that her breasts were large and full. He felt himself grow warm as desire, unexpected and overwhelming, roared through him.

He stepped back, out of her possible line of vision, and tried to calm his body's response to the sight of her. He couldn't rejoin his party with anything resembling the hard-on that was threatening his peace of mind and his equanimity, not to mention the front closure of his slacks. He inhaled deeply and turned away from her to look at the artwork around him, trying to lose himself in the variety. When his body calmed, he turned sharply and walked away to the place he knew his colleagues had taken the students. Both of them were female, and the younger one eyed him speculatively, as though she knew something had transpired and only needed to look at him to be able to sum up his experience. The older one ignored him as she always did.

The students who had chosen to come on this tour were listening to the docent talk about the pieces in the gallery, and Peter paid as little heed as he needed to give the semblance of attention while his body remained totally aware of the fact that the mystery woman was once again occupying the same building as he was.

Is she an Englishwoman? Is she on holiday ... again? Who is she?

When the docent moved on, he did, too, and found himself in the same gallery as his mystery lady once more. Her profile greeted him this time, and he fought to keep his eyes off her and on the works the guide was describing. He closed his eyes and breathed away the tightness in his chest. *This is ridiculous,* he thought angrily, and was about to turn resolutely away when her scent assailed him.

He was shocked to discover that he remembered it from that one brief meeting two months earlier. It had imprinted itself on his synapses, setting off electrical pulses that made his skin tingle with awareness, and his heart race. He looked around and discovered he didn't have to look too far down to see into the most incredible coffee-brown eyes. The woman glanced up, and he knew she recognized him by the way her eyes widened. He felt obliged to speak, though he was at a loss as to what to say.

"Hello again," he settled for, smiling faintly. He felt like a child, gawking longingly at candy in the shop window. He wished he knew why this woman brought out such odd and unsettling reactions in him.

"Oh, hello! Small world!" she replied, her smile a nervous reflection of his own.

"Yes, isn't it?" *What an utterly inane response!* "Are you on holiday?" The question popped out without his permission, and he closed his eyes briefly, opening them again expecting there to be a sharp reprimand for his temerity.

Instead, the woman smiled at him and answered, "In a way, I suppose I am. My brother lives here, and I have just moved from the States. I'm a writer and freelance editor looking to enlarge my clientele. I'm taking in the sights and soaking up the culture." Her smile widened charmingly, then she stuck her hand out and added, "My name is Karen, by the way. Karen Mullings."

"Peter van der Meulen," he said, taking her hand in his.

It was velvet smooth, and very soft, the dark pigmentation of her skin tone contrasting warmly with his paler one. She was beautiful close up with dimples in her cheeks and a sexy mole above the left corner of her top lip. She had a few freckles scattered across her cheekbones, a fact that surprised him as he had thought only very pale people had them.

"It's very nice to meet you again," he added, reluctantly relinquishing her hand.

"Are you on holiday?" she asked in her turn.

"In a manner of speaking," he returned with a laugh. "A busman's holiday. My colleagues and I have brought some students over on a school trip. It's an annual event in our school." Immediately after he said it, he remembered why he was in the museum. "Which reminds me, I'd better catch up with my group." He paused, then decided to go ahead and take the plunge. "But if you'd like some company, how about a drink later this evening?"

Karen didn't respond immediately. In fact, she appeared not to have heard him, and he was just about to repeat himself when she spoke up.

"I'd like that. Thank you." She gave him the name of her hotel, which he recorded in his handily secreted notebook.

"Eight o'clock good for you? We have to see to the students first."

Karen smiled, her dimples flashing at him. "Eight will be fine. Thank you."

Peter felt himself drowning in her eyes and clenched his hands into fists behind his back to bring himself back from the edge.

"I'm sorry, but I must rush off now," he said. "See you at eight."

For the rest of the afternoon, Peter was distracted, and it showed. Neither of his colleagues had witnessed his meeting with Karen, and he was glad of that, but he kept expecting the younger one, Anika, to accost him about his inattention. While she did look at him questioningly a time or two, she refrained from commenting, for which he was grateful, as he could not even think of a good lie to explain away his behavior. Mina, the older one, steadfastly ignored him. He suspected it was because he had snubbed her once when she seemed to be making advances he was not interested in accepting.

Mercifully, the tour ended, and they took their twelve students, along with the eight from the other group and their other colleagues, Miep and Jan, out for dinner at a local eatery in the neighborhood where the host families' homes were located. He managed to keep his attention on his companions during the meal, enjoying the students' buoyant spirits as they made amusing observations about the other patrons in the restaurant, about their teachers, and about each other. He had been lucky to be assigned to this particular group of students, all of whom were level-headed, intelligent, and witty. His colleagues he tolerated, as he did most of them at work, and they got along because they tolerated him as well.

There were very few people whom Peter trusted, but he managed to get along with everyone, mostly because he made himself invisible. He rather liked being the one most people overlooked, especially after Alijd's death, when the natural reaction of his peers had been to smother him with attention in an attempt to keep him from brooding. Little did they know how odd his grief had been, and that he had been grieving her loss for years before she died.

He shook himself out of his reverie in time to participate in the review of plans for the next day. After more walkabouts, including enjoying the changing of the guard and the march along the Mall back to Buckingham Palace, they would return to their host families, participate in a local fun fair on Friday morning, and have the afternoon and evening to themselves. On Saturday, they were to return to Leeuwarden.

He saw that Karen was staying at the Tavistock Hotel, close to the Museum where they had met again. It seemed they were staying close to her. He asked directions of the father of their host family and was even given leave to borrow the family sedan to take himself off for his date.

CHAPTER 2

P romptly at eight, after having left far too early and spending most of the extra twenty minutes finding a flower shop and making a purchase, Peter knocked on the door of room 413. He waited a heartbeat before the door opened and Karen appeared, a smile lighting her face.

"Please come in!" she invited him, and when he stepped inside, she closed the door and turned back to say, "What beautiful flowers! And how thoughtful of you to have brought them in a vase!"

"I'm glad you like them," he replied, handing them to her with a smile of his own.

He watched her walk over to the table beside the couch and push aside the books on it to place the flowers. Her hips were wide, her bottom round and inviting, and he felt his body stirring at the sight. He was glad in that moment that he was standing in the shadowed entryway, so she wouldn't notice if his cheeks heated from the direction of his thoughts. He had to get a grip!

"I noticed the hotel has quite a serviceable bar," he said hastily to distract himself. "We can go there, or I can take you to a quiet little pub I noticed a few blocks away. It'll be a nice walk if you're up to that!" His eyes went to her feet, which were encased in high-heeled pumps.

She noticed where he looked and chuckled. "I'll manage," she answered. "These are my work shoes!"

She walked toward him, holding a small clutch that matched the sunshine yellow of her dress. He loved a woman in a dress, and he swallowed against the urge to stare at her pretty legs beneath the knee-length skirt. He could not withhold the compliment that burst from his lips, however.

"You look lovely, Karen!" The warmth of his comment shone from his eyes, and Karen's face heated in response.

"Thank you! You look quite dapper yourself!" She walked through the door he opened for her, and waited until he closed it before asking, "So, have you decided where we're going?"

"I believe I have," he answered and escorted her down to the lobby. "I noticed it during one of our day tour walks," he said. "It looks quite cozy and not too crowded. Shall we?"

He gave her his arm, and they strolled the few blocks to the pub. By the time they got there, Peter had worked up an appetite and hoped she wouldn't mind sharing supper with him. He waited until they were seated at a small table in the back before asking, "Could you use some supper?"

"I don't mind if I do," she replied with a smile.

"What would you like to drink?" he wanted to know next and went to give their order and ask after a menu. Returning with the drinks, he put her glass of Riesling before her and sat with his own glass. "Perhaps we can share a fish and chip supper? They seem to be rather large servings."

"That would be fine," she said, sipping her wine and smiling at him.

He gestured for a waiter and placed their order, then turned back to her to say, "Whereabouts does your brother live?"

"Birmingham," she answered. "He's away on business, and I didn't fancy staying alone, so I took the opportunity to come down to London for a visit till he comes back."

"I'm rather glad you did," he said and took a large swallow of wine.

He didn't know what was coming over him, but he was almost garrulous, not at all his usual reserved self. Something about this woman sitting across from him stirred him up and disturbed his quiet equilibrium. It was at once exhilarating and disconcerting, and as he watched her sip her drink, he wondered how he was going to get it under control. If he could get her to talk, it might shut him up

"So, why would you wish to leave the States to live in a smaller country?" he wondered and made room for the food that the waiter brought just then.

Karen waited until she had served her plate before replying, nibbling on a fat chip. "I'm a small-town island girl. The States was just too big, too overwhelming. Everything was larger than life, overblown, and after my first visit here, I knew this was where I wanted to live. I wanted to get back the feeling of being home." She cut a piece of the fish on her plate and ate it.

"And home is ...?" Peter watched her eat and had to remind himself not to stare.

"Jamaica," she answered.

"Ah," he said, taking a forkful of the fish before him. "I thought I heard a bit of an accent!"

"Have you visited Jamaica?" Karen asked, sipping her wine again and eyeing him speculatively.

"No," he answered, "but I have a friend who is married to a Jamaican, and I sometimes visit them when I'm in England on my own." He paused, swallowing more wine before adding, "Your accent isn't as heavy as hers, though. That's why I couldn't place it." He smiled at her and returned his eyes to his plate, stuffing chips and fish into his mouth to keep from saying more.

"That's probably because I was born there but spent my growing up years on a different island," she commented with a chuckle. "I'm a truly Caribbean child because I lived on a third island as a young adult before moving to the States."

"Ah, you're a well-traveled lady, then," he said, watching her face.

"I wouldn't say that," she replied, "because aside from a month-long stay in the south of

France when I was a girl, my visit to Amsterdam was my first visit to the European continent."

The conversation meandered among various other light, getting-to-know-you topics as they ate, and Peter ordered a second round of drinks, this time an Amaretto sour for her at her request, and a Drambuie for himself. He let himself relax completely, watching her as she watched the other patrons in the pub. Her face was serene as though she had a wellspring of calm inside her. He wanted to know how someone could be so calm in such uncertain circumstances. She didn't have a nine-to-five job, and she was living with her brother, a condition he felt certain she would not long endure. She seemed to be pretty independent, and he found he liked her spunky attitude.

"I often wonder what people find so enticing about pubs," she said, "to make them return every day." She turned to look at him briefly before turning her gaze back over the crowded room.

"I suppose it's a socializing spot," he said. "It's where their friends are, where they can relax after a long day, where they can play."

"I understand that," she replied, "but I don't get the drinking. Why drink so much that they leave at least buzzed and often drunk? What's the pull?"

She sounded genuinely puzzled, and it occurred to him that she might be more inexperienced than she appeared to be, and for some reason, it drew him to her more.

"I take it you're not a frequenter of pubs, then?" he asked, smiling, having no answer to her question.

"I can count on the fingers of one hand the number of times I've been in a bar with fingers left over," she answered on a laugh. Then, as if it occurred to her that he might think she was unhappy with having been brought to a pub, she hastened to add, "Not that I'm complaining about where we are. Please don't misunderstand me!"

Peter saw the faint blush on her cheeks and knew she thought he might be offended at her words. Her concern for his feelings did something to him inside, and he had to struggle not to react. He merely smiled, nodded, and finished his drink, raising his hand for the check.

"Nevertheless, perhaps it's best that we go now. I have a full day of touristy things lined up tomorrow with the students, and the day after, it's back home for us."

Karen waited until they were once again strolling down the sidewalk back to her hotel before repeating the same question he had asked her earlier.

"And home is ...?"

"Leeuwarden," he answered, "about two hours away from Amsterdam."

"My knowledge of The Netherlands, before my visit to Amsterdam two months ago, is limited to what I learned in geography class as a girl in high school, and what I read in Betty Neels' novels." She chuckled merrily.

"Betty Neels?" he inquired, steering her round an obstacle in their path.

"A writer of romance novels back when I was a girl," she replied. "Her heroes were always impossibly tall, handsome, and virile Dutch doctors or consultants, and her heroines were always English nurses or other caregivers. Many were Plain Janes, in their own eyes at any rate, but every once in a while, she had a raving beauty as a heroine. I loved her stories," she added. "They were sweet and tender, no sex scenes at all, and maybe only one or two hot kisses, but lots of suggestive sensuality. They were good for a teenage romantic who had no interest in sex or descriptions of it at the time."

Peter smiled. He loved that she was sharing something of herself with him. "Sounds like something that could happen," he said. "The Dutchmen and the English women, I mean. We like traveling to England."

Karen smiled back at him, a twinkle of amusement in her eyes. "English girls not as feisty as Dutch girls?" she asked and was rewarded with a laugh.

"I don't know about that, but I do know we enjoy the English landscape. It's unlike ours, which as you know is flat, and yet it can often be a comforting reminder of home."

"Betty Neels married a Dutchman herself," Karen added, "so she must know something of their character. Enough to make her replicate them in her stories, although her husband had been a sailor, not a doctor."

They walked the rest of the way in companionable silence, and at her door, he waited until she had opened it before saying, "Thank you for accepting my invitation. I had a lovely evening."

Karen smiled up at him. "So did I." Her smile was suddenly shy, and his heart skipped a beat.

"When are you leaving London?" he asked, acutely aware of her breast close to his arm, and of her soft breathing, and of the fact that he didn't want to leave her.

"I go back on Sunday," she said, her eyes suddenly wistful before she lowered them from his gaze.

There was a short pause during which neither spoke nor looked at the other. It was awkward, and neither seemed to know how to break it. Then Karen stuck her hand out, breaking the spell that had them caught in its grip.

"It was nice meeting you again," she said. "Have a safe trip home."

Peter took the proffered hand and held it, not moving or speaking, trying to process the thoughts that whirled in his brain. He didn't want to leave, but of course, he had no choice. He wanted to stay in contact with her but couldn't think how to do that. He'd have to figure it out before Saturday morning. He became aware that he was still holding her hand, and he let himself register the feel of her soft skin again before releasing her.

"Thank you! I hope you find a job soon. Take care!"

A brief smile, and he turned on his heel before he did the most outrageous thing imaginable and kissed her. They were still strangers, and his libido would not be excused for taking such a liberty. He could feel her eyes on him as he walked away, and he only managed to let out the breath he had been holding when he rounded the corner to get to the elevator. The whole way home he wrestled with how to stay in touch with her, and by the time he got to his room, he had a plan.

CHAPTER 3

The next day, during the break for lunch, Peter excused himself on the pretext of running an errand and took a cab to Karen's hotel, where he left a note for her at the front desk. Satisfied that he had done all he could, he returned to his group and spent the rest of the morning and early afternoon wearing himself out on the activities they had planned. He took the requisite pictures of the sights and of the students but found he was subdued, almost listless by the time they returned to their host homes, despite the evident good time that his group had at the fun fair.

The one bright spark of his day had been the purchase he had made in one of the stalls of a pretty crystal pendant suspended on a length of leather. He could see it hanging on a silver chain around Karen's neck, nestled in her cleavage, drawing eyes to her generous bosom. He knew it had probably been a stupid thing to do, buying such a personal gift for a stranger, but he had submitted to the impulse and could not find it in his heart to regret it even after he had some time to think about how, if ever, he would get it to her and whether or not he would purchase a chain to go with it also. He excused himself from dinner, pleading a headache, and sat next to the window in his room, staring out over the street.

That one woman could so unsettle him after all the years of emotional drought with Alijd in the last years of their marriage, then after her death, was startling to him. He had assumed his chance had passed, and he would never again feel the stirrings that were now driving him crazy. He wished he could go back to room 413 and ... what? The thought of the things he wanted to do to a woman he didn't know made him grimace with frustration and embarrassment. If she knew where his thoughts strayed to, she would run a thousand miles from him.

He sighed and finished his packing, then sat down to write a letter, the first of many he suspected, to Karen Mullings. It felt like a necessary thing to do, and it took him an hour to say all that was on his mind at the moment. After he had sealed it in an envelope and slid it into the secret pocket of his suitcase, he changed and went to bed. He had no idea how he would ever send it to her, assuming he was bold enough to try, but it had helped to relieve his mind of the thoughts swarming through it so he could rest well. They would need to be up early in the morning for a long day of traveling, and he would rather not be tired for the journey from a lack of sleep.

By Saturday afternoon, while Peter was on the last leg of his journey home, Karen had been out and about in a kind of stupor. She had no intention of letting the curious lethargy and its accompanying feeling of letdown ruin her unplanned mini holiday. She had gone to another museum, taken a boat ride on the Thames, braved the London Eye, toured the Tower of London, and was finally back in her room, exhausted and hungry. She took a shower and sprawled on top of the cool sheets clad only in an oversized T-shirt and panties. She thought about the note that Peter van der Meulen had left at the front desk for her. His handwriting was so ... European, she mused as she reached over to snag it from the side table and re-read it.

"Dear Karen," it read, *"I cannot help but think it serendipitous that we bumped into each other again after so long a time apart. I don't know why we met again, but I find myself grateful that we did. I would like to stay in touch if that's alright with you. This is my number at home, and my cell phone number, should you wish to call."* She skipped over the numbers. *"Or, if you prefer, drop me a line. I'll be sure to respond whichever way you use to contact me. Have a lovely weekend! Peter."*

His email address was also in the note, and she wondered, as she put it back on the table, what his home address was, and if he lived in a house or an apartment. And then she wondered, with a frown, why she was wondering where he lived. It was a bit presumptuous of him to suppose she would be interested in keeping in touch with him, but she acknowledged at the same time that, given the way she had felt all Thursday evening in his company, if he were in the same condition, his note was very restrained. She lay back, wishing for sleep to overtake her, wishing she knew why she felt as though her dog had died. After an hour of tossing and turning, she fell into a fitful slumber, from which she was awakened by her cell phone's drumming alarm, waking her for dinner.

She dressed in slacks and a button-down shirt and, on a whim, went back to the pub where she had dined with Peter. It was much more crowded, but she managed to find a space to sit in the back and sipped the soft drink she had ordered while her fish and chip supper was made. People came and went over the next hour, while she ate her solitary meal and tried to soak up the ambiance. Once or twice, she thought she caught someone looking at her, but when she returned her gaze to him, he was looking elsewhere. She wasn't frightened by the scrutiny and wished he would come over and say hello. Although she had no interest in a relationship, she didn't mind company.

She ordered a glass of wine with dessert, and as she ate, she thought about how she could possibly meet Peter again. The second meeting, like the first, had been sheer coincidence, and there was absolutely no hope of its being repeated. Her musings were interrupted by a deep voice in her ear.

"I like a woman who doesn't mind her own company," it said, an amused undertone sounding in it.

Karen looked up into the blackest eyes she had ever seen and recoiled as though she had been stung. "I beg your pardon?" Her voice was cold, aloof, unwelcoming.

The man smiled and sat down. She bristled. "I don't recall inviting you to sit down," she commented acerbically.

"Sorry, lass, but I'm too tired to cross swords with you. I need a seat, and there's one here." His voice remained amused as though she were a toy meant for his entertainment. She drew her brows together and sat up.

"I would have thought common courtesy would dictate that you at least ask if I mind!" she snapped.

"If courtesy were that common, we'd all have it. Now calm down and eat your tart." He flashed a smile at her and put out his hand. "I'm Niall, by the way, Niall McLaren. And you are...?"

Karen was tempted to say, "Leaving," but she bit back the retort as she wasn't ready to leave just yet. Against her better judgment, against all common sense (he was right, if it were so common, everyone would have it, and she clearly didn't!), she was intrigued by this brash stranger. She liked the way his full lips curled up when he smiled, the way his eyes twinkled with amusement, the cleft in his chin. She liked his broad shoulders and bulging biceps. Maybe he would help take her mind off Peter van der Meulen, who was as fair as Niall was dark, and as different from him as night from day. However, she wasn't about to give him her name just like that.

"I am debating the wisdom of giving my name to a stranger!" she retorted and watched his face. When he burst out laughing, she couldn't hold back the grin that creased her cheeks.

"Good one, lass!" he said, keeping his hand outstretched.

Karen took it and felt her hand gently engulfed in a big, warm grasp. "I'm Karen Mullings," she said. "Are you satisfied now, Mr. McLaren?"

"Niall, please," he invited her. "And yes, it satisfies me to know your name." He raised the stein of beer to his lips and drank deeply before continuing, "You've been the subject of some speculation this evening. Did you know that?"

Karen sipped her drink and looked at him curiously. "No, I didn't. Who was speculating and why?"

"I heard one man to say you didn't look like a woman who had just been dumped by her lover," he said, watching her face as he drank his beer.

"Lover? What on Earth ...?"

"Were you here last evening?"

"Yes, with an acquaintance." Karen looked into Niall's black eyes and smiled. "In fact, I bumped into him for the second time two days ago at the British Museum. We came here for a drink and a late supper." She chuckled before adding, "You have the distinction of being only 50% less well acquainted with me than he is." Niall chuckled with her, and she noted a look come and go in his eyes. "What?" she asked him.

He didn't pretend not to know what she meant. "You are a very beautiful woman, Karen," he said. "Any man who would dump you is either blind or stupid or both."

"If beauty were the only reason for keeping me, it wouldn't be enough, surely?" she argued reasonably, amused by his observation. She was not a vain woman. "No one remains beautiful for life."

"I beg to differ," he said. "Beauty is not just about what you look like on the outside."

"And how would you know then, on the basis of one meeting, that I am beautiful on the inside?" she retorted, laughing at him.

He was silent for a long moment, taking another swallow of beer, regarding her with serious eyes. When he spoke, his words held quiet conviction. "It's very easy to see the beauty inside you," he said. "It's in your intelligence, your feistiness, your sense of humor. It's in the way you look directly at others, in the way you stick to your guns, and do only what feels right to you. That's beautiful!"

Niall watched her blush and lower her eyes and wished he could know her better. He had also seen her with the unknown man the night before, and something told him not to try for her, even though right now he wanted to take her away from the eyes he could feel on them, somewhere quiet, somewhere private, so he could take what he knew she would not give him as easily as she had given him her name. She was different from most of the women who threw themselves at him, and he found he wanted to spend time with her, sharing her quiet good humor and her unique view of the world.

"As this is only the second time I've noticed you here, I assume you're not from around here," he observed.

"And you'd be right," she replied and sipped her drink.

Niall grinned at her. She was feisty for sure. She wasn't about to give him any more information than she thought he needed, and it made him want to reach across the table and kiss her. But that wouldn't get him any closer to his goal, so he let it go. No matter what happened, he was determined to get to know this woman. At the very least, he wanted to be her friend. He sensed that she would be a steadfast and loyal one.

"I'd hate to think we met too late," he murmured.

"Too late? For what?" Her gaze was quizzical.

"For us to become friends," he answered. "If you're going home, how can that happen?"

Karen studied his face for a long minute, and Niall found himself feeling nervous. She had an unwavering gaze, and it pinned him like a specimen under a microscope.

"Are you sure it's only friendship you're interested in, Niall?" she asked finally, her face and voice serious.

The question did not surprise him, nor did he evade it. "Obviously, since I am a red-blooded male, I wouldn't object to there being more, but going there at this point would be premature, don't you think? I'm sure you've heard enough pick-up lines to last your lifetime, and I'm not in the market for a quick fix."

He drained his beer stein and stood up, suddenly needing to put some space between them. "Would you like another?" he asked, indicating her empty glass. "I need another pint."

"No, thank you," she answered.

"Will you be here when I get back?" he wanted to know, his question serious.

Karen smiled. "If you like," she said.

He returned her smile, liking her more every second. "I'll be quick, then."

Karen watched him walk away. He was a big man, a little taller than Peter, and wider, though she didn't see any surplus fat anywhere on him. He must be at least six inches over six feet. She cast her eyes around the room and observed a number of women watching him as he laughed at something the bartender said and smiled with a patron sitting at the bar. She watched them watch him walk back to her, his strides long and measured and confident. She watched their eyes take in his smile as he sat down again and took a long swallow of his drink.

"Apparently, you're getting your fair share of attention as well," she commented with a grin. "I can see why, too."

Niall cocked an eyebrow at her. "Why?" he wanted to know.

"I have a friend who would describe you as a 'chick magnet'," she returned and laughed when he choked on his beer, narrowly missing spewing a mouthful all over the table. She watched him clean up the mess with the napkins on the table and swallow again before he answered her.

"Interesting," he said and inhaled deeply. "Then I guess we're even."

Now it was Karen's turn to stare inquiringly at him. "How so?"

"I watched all the men watch you last night," he said, "and again tonight. They can't keep their eyes off you. And if I don't miss my guess, I know exactly what they're thinking, too."

A small silence greeted his words, then she said, "How can you be so sure about what they're thinking? Is it because it's what you're thinking, too?"

It was a challenge, and Niall was never one to back down. "I wouldn't insult your intelligence by pretending otherwise," he admitted. "But the difference between me and the rest is that I'm prepared to take 'No' for an answer and not hold it against you." He paused, waiting for his words to sink in. "I meant what I said about being a friend."

Karen remained silent, only nodding her head to acknowledge that she heard him. She needed to go as she had to get an early bus back to Birmingham, but she was really enjoying Niall's company. She found his honesty delightfully refreshing but wished he had not come to further complicate her emotions. Niall was a lot like her dear friend Jake, whom she had loved, though not enough to marry. With time, she could fall for him as surely as she could fall for Peter. The last thing she needed was two men vying for her attention. She had never been very good about making decisions like this. She hadn't been good at getting out of her engagement to Jake because she hadn't been able to choose the right time or the right words for letting down a man who clearly loved her in a way she had never loved him. Because she had been a coward then. Two men now was too many.

"I'm afraid I'll have to call it a night," she said finally. "I have to catch an early bus tomorrow."

Niall watched her rise to go and pay the check. He said nothing, letting her go, but watching until he saw she was ready to leave. He stood with his glass in hand and walked toward her, escorting her out of the crowded room. They stood together on the sidewalk under the bright green awning.

"Thanks for enlivening the end of my evening out, Niall," she said on a smile. "It was nice talking with you."

"I'm glad I was pushy, then," he said, and smiled down at her. "Take care of yourself, until we meet again, Karen."

Karen hid her smile at his comment. How they would meet again she didn't know, nor was she going to ask. But she admitted to liking his ebullient spirit and to wishing she were not just a visitor. He might make a good friend, indeed. She shook his hand and walked away, thinking how funny life is. A year ago, she had been so wounded in spirit she never thought she would recover. Resigning her position in the high school, selling her condo, and moving to England had all been part of her "take back my life" plan. But she had not expected to ever find any man even remotely interesting and had not met anyone at all ... until two months ago. And now, suddenly, there were two men. She shook her head ... it probably meant nothing and was merely coincidence.

She was forty years old and used to men wanting her. Truth be told, she was used to men being bold and pushy with her. She had been proposed to three times, the last time by a man she thought was joking. He hadn't been, although her acceptance had been, and when he was killed in an accident a year ago, the relief she felt at not having to marry him filled her with grief and guilt in equal measure. She just wasn't sure of herself where men were concerned anymore. Her experiences with them had not been the kind to instill confidence in her ability to read them or to meet them at their point of need. She felt a little broken, almost, so this double assault was leaving her feeling off kilter.

Niall McLaren watched Karen walk away from him. After a moment of indecision, he took the half-finished beer back inside, paid his tab and hurried out, hoping he would not miss her. He hustled along in the direction she had taken and almost passed her by. She had stopped in a little boutique that sold scarves and potpourri. He waited a moment, then strolled in after her.

"I'm glad I caught you," he said from beside her. "I realize I have no way of contacting you, should I wish to, nor did I give you any way to contact me."

Karen swung her eyes to his face, a frown creasing her brow. She hadn't expected him to follow her and was grateful she had stopped instead of going all the way to her hotel. She didn't want him knowing where she was staying, even if she was leaving in the morning. She was too unsettled by the whole situation to want more contact so soon.

"I'll leave you a number that you can call if you're ever in the area again ... how's that?" Niall suggested, noticing her hesitation and bailing her out. He didn't want her to feel obliged to give him information she wouldn't otherwise give. He extracted a business card from his wallet and handed it to her after scribbling his personal cell phone number on the back.

"I do hope you'll find a reason to use this," he said, his face and voice serious.

"Thank you." Karen smiled tentatively at him and watched him leave the shop. She waited a full ten minutes before leaving herself, after purchasing some potpourri for her room in her brother's house. Perhaps the next time she visited London she would give him a call.

CHAPTER 4

By the time Karen was sitting in the bus waiting for it to leave the station for Birmingham, Peter had been back home for more than twelve hours and had just got up to make himself a cup of tea. He knew it was far too early to be up on a Sunday morning, but he couldn't sleep, and thought he might as well get out of bed. He sat at the old grand piano in his living room and trailed his fingers across the keys. It had been a while since he'd played the piano, preferring to fuss with the violin sitting on the rocking chair in the corner. He was a far better pianist than he was a violinist, but he loved the little instrument and was always trying to improve his performance on it.

Now, though, he needed the certainty he felt with the ivory under his fingers. The piano was his last resort when he needed to think, and because he knew why he had had a disturbed night, he knew he needed to think. He sipped his tea, then put the cup on the seat beside him and let his fingers go where they would. The piece he began to play was a favorite of his, one that he found very moving. The mellow sounds flowed into the room, soaring and winding their way into his troubled spirit, making him feel at peace for the first time since he and Alijd had drifted apart.

Theirs had been a good relationship, despite Alijd's reluctance to take risks or try new things, even in the privacy of their bedroom. But the closer she got to forty, the more reserved she had become until she had no longer wanted his touch. Now, he was starved for passion, for the simple touch of a woman who wanted him. Maybe that was why Karen Mullings drew him like a moth to a flame—because he could see so clearly the passion she held inside her like a beacon. He wondered if she knew how deeply she had affected him and decided, as he switched from the mournful tune he was playing to a song of celebration, that he would step back into the light and let himself feel again.

The grandfather clock in the hall chimed the hour, and he got up, throwing out his cold tea in the kitchen sink and making a fresh cup. He sipped it slowly while he decided how to spend his day. Half-term was over, and tomorrow he would begin again. His students had all finished the last unit rather successfully, even the laziest and most mediocre of the lot, and the next unit was one where he was free to use his own resources to supplement the texts and videos agreed upon in the English teachers' meetings. Maybe he should start with a writing task ...perhaps a reflection on a quotation based on the next unit's theme. He would need to do a little searching, but that would not take up more than an hour of his time. He'd do that later. Right now, he felt the need to breathe in the air and dust away the cobwebs.

After hurriedly dressing in loose sweats and a t-shirt, he stepped out to the back porch to fetch his chocolate Labrador, Scrooge, and took the happy dog for a brisk walk. The sun was just coming up when he started out, but by the time he got back, jogging the last few blocks, it had risen fully, and a sharp morning light enveloped the land. He fed and watered the dog, scratching him behind the ears before going in to shower and get ready for his day. He decided to visit his aged aunt Lammie, tucked away safely in the old folks' home about seventeen kilometers away, and after lunch, he'd take in the weekly chamber music matinee. It had been a few months since he'd indulged his love for music, and he felt the need for it now more than ever.

Taking a box of chocolates with him because he knew his ancient relative had a sweet tooth and loved the treats he brought her, he announced himself at the front desk and was ushered into the common room. He saw his aunt sitting there by herself, a book in her hands, staring out the French doors on her left. She turned her head as he approached, and the smile that lit her face warmed his heart. She was his favorite aunt, and at ninety-six, she was full of stories to occupy their time together if she chose not to probe into his own life.

Bending down to kiss her wrinkled cheek, he hugged her gently and sat next to her, offering her his little gift.

"What a lovely surprise, dear Peter! And you brought chocolates!" she enthused, and he could hear the smile in her thin voice as much as he could see it on her face.

"It's been a while since your last treat," he said with a smile. "I knew you'd like them again!"

After helping her open the box, he settled into the seat and asked her how she'd been since his last visit. He listened to her careful yet amusing recounting of the escapades of some of the younger members of the home, about the arrival of two new inmates, as she dubbed them, and noted the sadness as she recalled the death of one of her closest friends there. Her voice grew even more quiet as she told him how she had been the one to raise the alarm because she had been in her friend's room at the time of her death.

Peter held his aunt's hand, feeling it tremble with emotion. He saw the tears that slipped down her cheeks and used his handkerchief to wipe them tenderly away. He did not speak. He knew she didn't need words and was comforted by his presence and his care of her. He didn't let her know that he worried about her health. She seemed somehow frailer to him, and though he knew her age must surely be a contributing factor, he made a mental note to ask the head nurse about her current condition. She turned to face him suddenly, a caramel-filled confection in her fingers and her eyes full of inquiry.

"When are you going to bring another woman for me to meet, Peter?" Her voice was high and sharp, and she pierced him with her bright-eyed stare, the muted sorrow of the moments just past apparently forgotten.

He smiled, wondering how best to sidestep the question. He must have hesitated too long because she continued, "It's not good spending the rest of your life brooding, you know. Alijd wouldn't have wanted that when she cared about you!"

That comment brought his head up sharply. What did she mean by "when she cared?" What had she sensed? He had not shared any of the misery of his last years with Alijd with anyone, but he had always known that his Aunt Lammie was a very intelligent and observant woman. He decided to be vague, without making it appear so, and hoped she would cease her probing.

"I'm not really brooding, Aunt Lammie. I've just been very busy, and no one I've met has piqued my interest." He was not about to tell her about Karen Mullings.

She turned her beady eyes on him, and he felt the sharpness of their regard like a scalpel on flesh. He was more than relieved when a tinkling sound and a softly spoken message over the intercom reminded the patrons that it was time for their mid-morning tea break.

"Won't you join me for elevenses, Peter?" his aunt invited him and stood up. "We can have it on the lawn in the back garden."

He didn't mind spending the mid-morning refreshment time with her over delicate miniature sandwiches, scones, and Earl Grey tea. Today's sandwich offering was some sort of vegetable spread—shredded spinach mixed with mayonnaise, spicy mustard, onions, a touch of garlic, and black pepper. Although he wasn't a lover of mayonnaise, the mixture was tangy and spicy and delicious, and he remarked silently again on how good the food was in this home. He was glad that this is where his aunt had chosen to end her days.

"Take a couple of these sandwiches with you, Peter," she urged him when he was ready to leave. "If I know you, you have more planned for today than just a visit to your old auntie, and you need to keep your strength up!"

This was the ritual she followed every time he stayed for tea, and Peter laughed at her attempts. "I'll be fine, Auntie! Just let me hug you again and kiss your cheek. And promise me to take care of yourself!"

She accepted his gentle goodbye hug, presented each cheek for his kisses, and said, with a twinkle, "If I am to take care of myself, then why do I need to be here?"

Peter chuckled as he led her back indoors, then made his way to the front where he asked to speak with the head nurse. "I'm here about Lambertine van der Meulen," he told her, when she had ushered him into her office. "How is she doing?"

The short, buxom woman facing him across the desk smiled. "She's doing wonderfully well in the circumstances."

Peter said nothing, only waited for her to continue. He knew his aunt had some medical issues, but he wanted to know what else was going on with her.

"She hasn't been sleeping well lately, though, and the death of her very close friend Janneke van Vliet hasn't helped with that at all. Mevrouw van Vliet died in her sleep, but she had been very ill for a long time before that. I think your aunt is afraid to go to sleep at night now more than ever because she's worrying about being alone at night and dying in her sleep without anyone she loves with her."

"Is there anything to be done to help her?" he asked.

"Not more than give her sleeping aids, which we don't think she's taking. Perhaps you can ...?"

"I'll see what I can do to persuade her," he said, anticipating her request. "Thank you for your time," he added, rising to leave.

"No, thank you, Mijnheer van der Meulen! It's always a pleasure to have you visit!"

The woman rose and extended her hand, and Peter shook it politely, wondering why it felt as though he had had to almost forcibly retrieve it from her grasp. She was looking at him in a very odd way that he could not read, but he was satisfied it had nothing to do with his aunt's condition, so he dismissed it and drove away. Only later, as he was leaving the symphony hall after enjoying a most delightful and satisfying concert, did he see that same look again. He bumped into a woman he had dated a couple of times before he decided there wasn't enough between them to continue to see her, and it was there in her eyes. This time he recognized it for what it was. *Two women on the same day ... that must be some kind of record,* he thought with a chuckle as he drove home, then he sobered as he wondered how he would react if Karen Mullings looked at him that way.

The rest of the day was a blur of activity. He made some plans for the next few days of classes and generally got himself ready for work, walked the dog, wrote his second letter to Karen—wondering all the while why he was bothering—and after a late-ish supper and a shower, took himself off to bed. Next morning when he awoke with a start, the sheet beneath him and his body wet with cum, he wondered what had triggered the most erotic dream he could ever recall having had since he was a raw and hungry teenager. He certainly hadn't had a wet dream since then. He lay there panting, reliving the dream, wishing it were real.

He was sitting at the piano, playing a tune from one of his favorite composers, and Karen sat next to him on the stool, humming along. He could smell her perfume, and it was distracting him, as was her knee brushing his, and the soft sounds of her humming. He fought to control his need and the lust that raged in him. His hands trembled on the keyboard, and he struggled to keep them steady.

"You play really well, Peter," she said and smiled at him.

He shouldn't have looked at her. He knew it the minute he did because he saw the same rioting emotions in her eyes that were rocking him to his core. He stopped playing abruptly and turned to her, taking hold of her shoulder and demanding a response from her mouth which he took almost savagely. Their tongues dueled with each other hungrily, and when she moaned, he lost what little control he had completely.

He groaned, his cock a harsh reminder that he was alone in bed, with only his hand to minister to his needs. He knew he'd have to relieve himself again before he went to work, but he wanted to keep the memory of the dream in his mind as he showered. He rose from the bed, stripping as he went into his bathroom, and palmed his cock as he stood under the warm spray, remembering.

She was riding him, her big breasts swaying, her eyes closed, her mouth open in ecstasy. He sucked a nipple into his mouth as he thrust into her deepest core, loving the way her inner walls clamped around his hard cock, claiming him, owning him, taking him. She rose and fell with a feverish rhythm, as hungry for him as he was for her. He pulled her head down so he could kiss her, and they ate each other as they made love, his motion needing hers, hers needing his to complete the seduction. They went faster, taking each other's body, going deeper, and he felt her falling apart around him as he burst the banks of his control and shot cum into the heart of her. He could not stop his hips, and she fucked him in time to his wild plunges into her soaking center, both of them collapsing at the same time with harsh cries of completion.

Peter's hand filled with the cum that boiled up from his tight sac as he fell over the edge again in a hard orgasm. He leaned against the shower wall, spent, trembling, taking in deep gulps of air, needing the woman he had only met twice, but whom, it seemed, he was lusting after. Humiliation and elation warred in his heart as he steadied himself, deploring his lack of self-control but excited at the realization that his libido wasn't dead after all.

CHAPTER 5

P eter waited until his body calmed before washing quickly, wishing he could linger to savor the dream. But the job he was tied to for still many years to come meant he had to hurry through his morning routine and stuff a sandwich in his briefcase . Thankfully, the coffee machine had made his two cups, so he transferred them, with cream, to his thermos and hurried out. He'd have to drive today—cycling in his current state was not an option.

The day flew by. There were the first three hours of teaching, followed by a coffee break in which he sat and stared vacantly out the window of the teachers' common room, remembering Karen's scent, her smile, her sassiness in the pub, and wondering what she was doing back in Birmingham. Three more classes, and his day was done, but a scheduled meeting with parents from seven to nine meant he had to find a place to have dinner or suffer the uninspired fare they served on such evenings in his school. Opting for a quick meal in a restaurant he favored close by, he walked the five blocks to the Chinese eatery and took a seat with two other teachers from the school who invited him to join them. They were a pleasant enough couple, recently married and glowing with the depth of their new love.

"Hello, you two lovebirds!" he greeted them cheerfully. "Sure you want an old sod like me sitting with you for dinner?"

Willem and Diana Minke laughed as he sat down. They were an odd pair, by most standards, and no one had suspected that they were an item until invitations had been received for their wedding. Diana had moved over from England to teach English, and they had hit it off immediately, but no one had suspected that the friendliness had led to anything more. They exchanged vows before a small group of their family, close friends, and colleagues on a lovely late spring morning. The brunch reception meant everyone, including the very-much-in-love newlyweds, could spend the afternoon as they pleased and not have a whole day lost to one occasion.

Peter placed his order and chatted amiably with his two younger colleagues, watching them together and feeling an ache settle in his heart. He hadn't realized, until his first encounter with Karen, how much he missed having someone of his own to love and be loved by. He had thought his marriage to Alijd would last a lifetime, that his love would never fade. He had been wrong, and the failure tore at his heart even now as he watched the couple before him. He silently prayed that his friends would be spared whatever mistakes he and Alijd had made to bring an end to the love between them.

Eating gave him something to do other than mope about his lack of a love life. He chewed slowly to savor the flavors in the dishes before him. He shared a carafe of some soft drink with his table mates and reluctantly packed up the rest of his meal and headed back with them to school for the late sessions. Parents came and went in his classroom in a blur of activity and talking, and at last it was over. He had seen more parents this time than he normally did, and he took that to be a result of his having been assigned two new classes mid-year.

He sighed as he packed his things and walked to the car. More and more he felt the need to change his job. He had been eyeing several positions in a couple of places in Haarlem, Groningen, and one or two other cities, and had more than half decided to try for them. They wouldn't need him before the autumn term if he applied and was hired, but it was certainly something to think about, to give him a reason to get up and do the same thing again the next day. At home again, he still had to walk the dog—poor Scrooge was whining with his need for relief—settle some bills, and prepare for the next day. After a quick shower, he wrote a sleepy note to Karen and saved it before rolling over to sleep.

He had decided that he would send them once she contacted him, ignoring the niggling fear that she would never call or write, and he would be stuck with some poetic twaddle that she might find embarrassing anyway. But he ruthlessly shrugged off the misgivings the next morning as he dressed for work. He felt a little green around the gills, but he supposed his body was merely protesting having to be back on a rigorous schedule. He grabbed his lunch and briefcase and hurried out to face another day. The rest of the week went by in a flurry of classes, staff meetings, and marking with little time left over for thinking too much about Karen. He did manage to write to her every night after walking Scrooge and showering before falling exhausted into bed.

Summer was almost upon them in Leeuwarden when Peter arrived home on a Friday evening after going out for drinks with friends from work to find a message on his answering machine.

"Hi Peter, this is Karen Mullings. Do you remember me? We last met at the British Museum, then went out for supper. I wonder if I might speak with you. Please call as soon as possible."

He listened to the number she gave him, writing it on the pad by the phone, then sat heavily in the chair next to it, his hands trembling slightly. He had almost resigned himself to never hearing from her again, so her call was a little shocking but very welcome. He wondered what she needed and hoped it was more than just information. Taking Scrooge for his walk helped to calm him, and by the time he sat down to write to her, he knew exactly what he would say when he spoke to her.

Across the English Channel, Karen sat up on her bed, the bedside lampshade tilted so she could see what she was doing properly and bit her lip. The story was stalled on the details she needed, and she had tried moving around it, but she knew whatever else she wrote might get changed if the details she wanted weren't supplied first. She didn't feel like rewriting anything on this one, so she saved the work done so far and closed the laptop. Then, on an impulse, she reopened it and opened her email. Maybe she should also send Peter an email asking what she needed to know, so they wouldn't need to talk. He could answer when he had a bit of time.

She knew, even as she typed his address in the "To" line, that she was finding reasons not to hear his voice again. Every time he had spoken, the husky, smoky texture of his voice had stroked her insides like a soft hand on tender flesh, and her tender flesh had become increasingly needy since meeting him. She didn't like being so out of control, and the fact that she had had to resort to artificial means to relieve the tension he had created upset her. She preferred her cocks live, and the toy she had finally given in and bought a few weeks previously, while it gave her the hard orgasms she craved, was not attached to the one man she found herself picturing in her mind every time she thrust its vibrating head into her aching flesh.

She had not been able to forget him, though she had to admit she had not really tried. Her brother George had returned from his business trip to find her pensive but had not been able to coax any explanations for it from her, despite their very close relationship. She hadn't known what to tell him, so she had kept silent. She hoped this feeling would pass, that she would get Peter out of her system before she exploded. She wondered, even as she began typing the email to him, what it would be like to have phone or cybersex with him. The thoughts made her panties dampen, and she knew she'd need her toy again if she was to get any sleep.

She quickly explained that she was sending the email because she might not be able to answer her cell phone when he called (what a lie!), and she was in rather a hurry to get the information. Would he please tell her all he could about which Dutch cities or towns were most at risk if a hurricane-like storm were to hit The Netherlands, and what the dangers were? She also needed to know if such a storm had ever hit, and what had been done, how much loss of life had there been, if any, and about damage to property. She explained that it seemed easier for her to ask him than to try to search on Bing or Google or some other search engine because, aside from the issue of having to sort through all the entries to find precisely what she needed, it had the added advantage of being an eyewitness account, as opposed to a clinical journalistic report.

She hit the "Send" button and inhaled deeply before putting the laptop away from her and lying back. She let her mind go over the last dream she had had of him that had awakened her so horny and desperate for him. She wondered if her hard and aching clitoris when she woke up was a smaller version of what it was like for a man waking to a hard-on. In her dream, he had escorted her to her door after a second date and was on his way back to his car when he had turned back suddenly and told her how much he had enjoyed the evening.

"I've missed your company. And I've wanted to kiss you since we first met. I can't leave this time without one!"

His eyes were on her mouth, and before she knew what was what, his hands were pulling her into his hard, aroused body, and she was kissing him back as ravenously as he was kissing her. Her arms went around his neck, and his hands held her body against his so she could not fail to feel the imprint of his desire on her aching flesh.

"Would you like to come in?" she had asked, dragging her mouth away from his before she gave in to the impossible impulse to beg him to take her on her front porch.

His nod was enough to get them through the door, which he had slammed impatiently behind them before grabbing her like a desperate man and feasting on her, pushing her up against the door and taking what she offered. When he raised her leg and his fingers had sought the wet flesh weeping for his touch, they had both groaned. And when he stroked her to her first orgasm, she had arched into his hand, and his mouth had stolen the harsh cry that rose from her throat. And when he had stripped her, still by the door, and pushed her up against it so he could send his hard rod plunging into her, she had fallen over the edge again before he took her flying a third time, roaring with his own release.

Karen reached for the toy she had hidden under the other pillows on her bed, thoughts of Peter van der Meulen filling her mind as she stroked herself, letting the vibrator play over her flesh through her soaked panties, wanting, even needing the pleasure to last. When she was almost at the point of no return, she lay it aside and stripped, getting back into the wide bed and this time sending it plunging to her wet depths, using her other hand to keep her clitoris stimulated, going harder and harder, sending the little toy to its highest setting and biting her lips to keep from howling when her orgasm overtook her. She kept plunging the rubber cock into her soaking center, needing something she knew in the small part of her brain that was not on a sex overload that it would never give her. It would never be enough. She needed flesh and blood.

Exhausted, she lay back, the tension easing from her limbs, the rubber toy still inside her, her heart slowing. She wished she understood why this one man had the power to drive her wild when she had only met him twice and knew nothing about him except what he did for a living. In fact, truth be told, he knew more about her than she did about him. The thought should have upset her, but she was too sated to care just then. Maybe once she woke up, she would. Instead, she dragged herself off the bed, changed the sheets and had a shower, cleaned her rubber lover, and placed it back under the pillows before going to sleep.

At breakfast next day, George told her she had missed a call from her friend Toni.

"Thanks, love," she said, kissing his cheek. "I'll call her later." She took her bowl of cold cereal to the table and added, "What? No work today?"

George chuckled. "I'm retired, remember? Any work I do is entirely up to me! I thought I'd take you for a drive today. You've been acting all pensive and moody, so I figured I owe it to you to help chase the gloom away." He sobered suddenly and said, "Look, I know you're worried about not having a proper job, love, at least, not the kind you thought you could get, but you've no need to worry. You can stay here as long as you like. You know that!"

Karen smiled at him. "I know, George. You and Elaine have been more than welcoming, and I appreciate it. But I'm forty years old. I need to be on my own again and soon!"

"Well, I've been looking into that, and as soon as I hear of something proper, I'll let you know, okay?"

"Okay," she said, and grinned at the thought of what he considered "proper" for his "little" sister. It was probably an apartment in someone's home with a huge dog and a high fence in a fancy part of town. "But I can't go out today. I need to get some more writing done. I'm on a roll. How about Wednesday?"

She decided to call Toni before getting back to her writing and was happy she didn't have to wait long for an answer.

"You're finally awake, eh?" Toni said when Karen greeted her. "Are you okay? You're not normally a late sleeper."

Karen rolled her eyes. Was everyone aware of the fact that things were out of whack with her?

"I'm fine. Just not sleeping well," she said, hoping the half-truth would be enough for her friend. Her hopes were dashed.

"Worrying about the job still?" Toni asked. "I could ask my boss..."

"No, you couldn't," Karen interrupted her. "Much as I find your job fascinating, it isn't for me." She chuckled and was relieved when her friend did, too. "I'll be fine, okay? Don't worry about me. As long as I can get this next book done by the deadline, I should be okay. Maybe I just need to wait for the royalties from the first one to start coming in and stop being so impatient."

"I know George isn't putting you out, so it's not housing you're really worried about. You know if I had room, I'd have you with me in a heartbeat!"

"I know, love, but I can't afford London at the moment, not for more than a few nights in a hotel." Her mind went immediately to her second meeting with Peter and to the dream that had sent her crashing last night.

"Well, the reason I was calling was to invite you to London for the weekend. I'm having a party for a friend who turns thirty on Friday. She's new in town, and I like her," she chuckled and added, "so I figure I'd introduce her around to other people I like. Will you come?"

"I can be there, but I'll have to see if I can find a reasonable room in a hotel close to you."

"You can stay with me, Karen. It's just for the weekend, after all. And anyway, if I'm not mistaken, I may be asked for a sleepover," she ended slyly.

"What's his name?" Karen asked on a laugh.

"Rory Stewart."

"Well, good luck with that. Will he be at the party?"

"Yes. It's a pity you don't know anyone to bring with you."

Karen's mind went immediately to Niall, and she said, without thinking, "As a matter of fact, I do. He lives in London, I guess. I have his cell phone number, and he asked me to call him the next time I was there. Shall I invite him?"

Toni whistled. "Keeping secrets from your old pal, are you?" she inquired, chuckling.

"He isn't a secret. I forgot about him, actually, until just now." Karen wasn't ready yet to share the reason Niall had been supplanted in her mind, so she added, before Toni could ask any questions, "As a matter of fact, I mentioned you to him when we met. I told him I had a friend who would describe him as a chick magnet."

"Ooooh! Is he that hot?" Toni wanted to know with a girlish giggle.

"If you like very tall, muscular, not-an-ounce-of-fat-anywhere hunks with mischief in their black eyes, yes!"

Karen laughed out loud when Toni said, "Get off the phone and call him now, girl! And then call me back and tell me what he said! And you'd better make sure he says yes!"

"What about Rory?" Karen asked, still laughing.

"What about him? He's coming, and he wants me so I'm almost certain he'll ask me over. That doesn't mean I can't enjoy the eye candy you bring with you. A girl has to keep her options open, you know." She paused, and then added, "You and he aren't...?"

"No, love, I've only met him one time!"

"But you have his number," Toni replied knowingly.

"Which means nothing more than he wanted me to stay in touch," Karen said.

"Which means he's interested in you," Toni retorted.

"Even so, it doesn't mean anything more, so don't worry about it."

"I don't want to poach, is all," Toni answered.

"Nothing to poach, love, so no worries!"

"Okay. Then get off the phone and call him. I'll be waiting for your message!"

Toni hung up immediately, and Karen laughed again. She could always depend on her friend to cheer her up. She went to find Niall's number and dialed, wondering how she would react when he answered, but there was no answer, and she was forced to leave a message. She said she would call back, then made an effort to get some work done. She had a deadline for the new story she was writing, and it was fast approaching. She hoped Peter would answer soon and ignored the rush of anticipation that accompanied that thought.

Halfway through the afternoon, when she was enjoying a cuppa with George and Elaine, who had gone shopping and had only come in a few minutes before, her cell phone rang. Her heart sped up, and she could feel her cheeks warming as she answered.

"Karen, it's Niall," the voice said. "How are you?"

Swallowing her disappointment—maybe she had only been interested in him because he had been there, a substitute for the man she really wanted—she said with false cheerfulness, "I'm fine, thank you. I'll be in London next weekend with my friend who is hosting a party, and she said I could invite someone. You're the only someone I know in London. Will you come?"

"Why, I'd be delighted to be your partner, Karen. Whereabouts in London? Will you need a ride to the party?"

"No, I'm staying in Toni's apartment," she said, searching for Toni's address and giving it to him. "Call this number if you need directions," she said.

Niall chuckled. "I'll find it. Never fear!" He paused, then asked, "You said you're staying with your friend Tony?"

"Antonia Larson," Karen clarified, smiling. She basked in the knowledge that he might be even a little jealous. She may not be interested in him, but it was still nice to know he was into her. "She's the one who will no doubt describe you as a chick magnet!"

Niall chuckled again. "I can't wait!" he said dramatically. "Nor can I wait to see you again!"

His voice had dropped on the last statement, and Karen waited for something to happen, for some reaction to the blatant seduction in his tone. Nothing. Zip. Zilch. Nada. She might as well have been talking to George. She knew she needed to say something, but she was suddenly as tongue-tied as a schoolgirl, though not for the reason he might assume if she didn't hurry up and speak.

"It'll be nice to see you again, too," she managed in a cool tone.

After she rang off, she wondered how the weekend would turn out but knew instinctively that Niall would never be the man to meet the needs that grew in her daily. She sighed, drawing Elaine's eyes to her.

"Problem?" she wanted to know.

"No," Karen answered. "Just thinking."

She excused herself and went back to writing, abandoning the story she had been working on in favor of one previously begun which she needed to finish as well, though it was on a much looser schedule. She would have missed dinner if Elaine hadn't come to dig her out of the cocoon of her room, and as soon as she had helped with the washing up, she withdrew again to finish the story. It was quite late, and she felt the need for a nightcap before turning in. The story not on a tight deadline was finally done to her satisfaction and only needed to be proofread, which she would do another day. The one for which she needed Peter's knowledge was still waiting, as was she, for some word from him.

As she poured herself a glass of wine and sat at the kitchen table, she wondered why she was getting upset that he had not called and why it mattered so much. Niall had called back within hours, yet here she was, a day later, still waiting to hear the voice of the man she knew she would not easily eradicate from her thoughts. It irritated her, even as she acknowledged that he might have responded to her e-mails, reading it as her sign that she would rather not speak to him. Which, if she were honest, it sort of had been.

She emptied the glass and filled it again, taking her drink with her back to her room. Getting back into life was difficult when she didn't know what she wanted, and she was finding it hard to figure it out. She knew one thing for certain. She wanted more than sex, even though she knew that was a big part of what would meet her need. She had had sex, lots of it, but she was still empty. She loved making love, but she wasn't about to settle for something that was only about scratching an itch when her heart and soul were crying out for more. Maybe she needed to figure out what would completely satisfy her before she allowed anyone, including the fascinating Peter van der Meulen, to make too great an impression on her.

She found Peter's answer as soon as she opened her e-mail. Would she mind an afternoon call tomorrow as he had an appointment this evening and needed to get some things done in the morning? She sent an affirmative response and sat in the darkness, watching the moon through the curtains, sipping the wine and wishing. It was hard not to hope when her body seemed to think that he might be the one, but she had learned pretty early on that men could be more vastly disappointing than anything and that a broken heart was the hardest thing to mend. Hers was pretty fragile as it was and still a little sore from its latest brush with disaster. She would be cautious, no matter what her body said.

CHAPTER 6

Peter woke early the next morning, lying in bed savoring the dream he had had. Not the wild sexual ride of recent dreams, this one had been sweet and romantic. He felt panic rising inside him at the thought that all along, in the last years with Alijd and the four since her death, he had been wanting the scene that had unfolded in his dream. Awake, he ran a mile from women and commitment ... life with Alijd in the last years of their marriage had been an increasingly miserable and eventually heartbreakingly impossible ride, and he wanted none of it. And knowing he wasn't a one-night-stand kind of man, he had deemed it better to steer clear of them and keep himself to himself. Now Karen had completely stirred him up, waking up all the dormant and powerful emotions he had buried in the deepest recesses of his heart when Alijd had rejected his love. And he couldn't seem to get them back under wraps.

They stared into each other's eyes, moving slowly to the music the band was playing. It was his cousin Maurice's wedding, and he had invited Karen as his date. She was radiant in a gold and black silk creation (were those the colors she had been wearing the last time they met?), *the sexy high heels bringing her almost eye level with him. She was smiling at something he had said, and her eyes glowed at him, making what was left of his defenses crumble into dust. He bent his head and touched his lips to her cheek, his hands trembling with a fierce need that had him swinging her off the dance floor and out onto the porch where he pulled her into his arms and kissed her soundly.*

"You are the loveliest woman here, and you have my heart, Karen," he whispered against her well-kissed lips. "Come home with me later, please, love!"

He waited until she nodded before kissing her again, losing himself in the sweetness of her breath and the warmth of her arms around him.

He took Scrooge for a longer walk than usual, wishing he could outdistance his troubled thoughts, but they remained with him even as he set food and water for the dog and went to shower. He had some errands to run in town and had promised to take a book to his Aunt Lammie that she had been wanting to read for some time. Then he would have lunch with her before coming back home to talk to Karen. He found he was growing more nervous as the morning wore on, and by the time he was sitting down to lunch in the residents' cafeteria with his ancient relation, he was a mass of nerves. His sharp-eyed aunt did not miss his discomfiture.

"Whatever's the matter with you, Peter? You're as skittish as a colt!" She eyed him worriedly, adding, with a chuckle, "A poor cliche, I know, but it seems most fitting in your case."

"I'm fine, Auntie," he answered and gave her half the truth. "I have a call to make that I'm a little nervous about, that's all."

"Well, as long as it doesn't interfere with pleasant conversation with my favorite nephew, feel free to indulge!" she said regally, a queen allowing her servant a treasured privilege.

Peter laughed and forced his shoulders to relax. He breathed in deeply, drank some water, and managed a fairly normal conversation with his aunt through the three courses of the meal.

As he was leaving, he kissed her cheeks and said, "Thanks for the lunch date, Auntie! I had a good time! Take care, okay?"

He squeezed her frail hands and smiled down at her, turning to walk away before the head nurse could accost him. He narrowly escaped her attention and grinned to himself as he drove off. The last thing he wanted was a meeting with the woman who it was now clear would make a pass at him if he let her. He stopped to buy tea and cream before finally going home. Once he had made himself a cup, he went into his office and picked up the phone. Karen was waiting, and he could no longer put off the inevitable. Besides, he had a stack of notes for her to read and needed to have an address to send them to. He would not examine the reason for the notes and would not face the possibility of rejection, at least not consciously. He'd cross that bridge when he got to it, but he was praying he could bypass it.

The phone rang twice before he heard her voice.

"This is Karen," she said. "How may I help you?"

"Karen, it's Peter," he replied. "It's so lovely to hear from you again. How are you doing?"

A small pause, then she answered. "I'm very well, thank you, Peter."

His name on her lips was a velvet caress, and he cleared his throat. "So, how can I help you?"

"Well, I'm writing a scene in which my characters are stranded in a city in The Netherlands by a storm with flooding, and I wanted an authentic, non-journalistic perspective on what that's like. I thought you'd be perfect for that."

Her voice was low, sultry, and though he knew instinctively that she wasn't trying to seduce him, he was enthralled by the sound anyway. "Well, I have experienced a few, yes. I'm happy to give you any information you may need."

They spoke for the next fifteen minutes, then she said, "Thanks, Peter. This is great!"

He could almost see the smile on her face, for he was sure he heard it in her voice. "I'm glad I could help," he answered, then hurried on. "I wonder if you would mind very much giving me an address to contact you. I've written some things I'd like you to read if you don't mind."

He knew he had been vague, but he didn't doubt that if she wanted more information, she would ask for it. So, when she did, he was not surprised.

"What sorts of things?" she wanted to know. "You didn't mention that you were also a writer!"

"Well, I'm not, in the way of being published or anything like that, but I have been writing a series of notes, as I call them, dedicated to someone special. I wonder if you could read them for me and critique them."

He wanted her to discover that they were all for her, and so increase her appreciation of the surprise of them and prayed she wouldn't be turned off by thinking he was asking her to read something meant for another. He could hear her hesitate, and wished he could see her face so maybe he could get a clue as to what she might be thinking. The moment stretched interminably, it seemed to him, and when she finally spoke, he let out the breath he had been holding unconsciously.

"Send them to my email address," she said. "I'll probably be moving soon, and I'd rather keep as little mail from my brother's mailbox as possible."

Was her voice cooler? Did he detect a wall going up? He could not be sure, and he rang off in a frenzy of uncertainty. As he had been saving the notes on his laptop, it was not hard to attach the file to an email after he transcribed the first one he had written on paper, while he was still in England, and saved it to the file. He sent it off immediately with an anxious prayer.

Two hours later, he received a response, and his heart leapt when he saw it. He had stayed online all afternoon, and now that it was here, he hurried to open it, fearing the worst, but hoping for the best, as they say. Her words leapt off the page at him, their meaning clouded for a time by his overwhelming relief that she had not rejected him. He read aloud to force his addled brain to concentrate:

Dear Peter,

> *I have never received a sweeter gift in all my life. I don't mind confessing that I was upset when you made your request, thinking you were asking me to read something you had written for someone else. It never occurred to me that it might have been for me as we have barely met twice and know so little about each other. So, when I read these precious notes and read your thoughts and feelings, I was humbled and flattered. It has taken me this long to send this reply because it has taken me this long to open your email. I promise to be more technical in my critique in the next message. This one is simply to say thank you. I am honored by your regard.*

Warmly,
Karen

She is so formal, he thought as he re-read the message, and somehow he knew it meant she was holding her emotions in check. Perhaps he could dare to hope that she was as overwhelmed by thoughts and feelings for him as he was for her. He sent a quick reply:

Dear Karen,

> *I am relieved that you are neither offended nor angry with me for presuming that you would have an interest in my thoughts. There is no hurry to read them. There will always be more. I'll explain the next time we are able to speak to each other. As you know better than most, sometimes writing it down isn't enough.*

> *Have a lovely evening.*
> *Peter*

He made himself shut down the laptop after that and found things to do to occupy his time until he went to bed, though not before writing another note for the woman he now happily knew would not reject his thoughts.

Karen lay back, her laptop on her belly, re-reading the notes Peter had shared with her. They were all written to her and dated. Her eyes misted over when she saw that he had been writing to her since their date in London. Clearly, she had made as deep an impression on him as he had made on her. She wondered why he had started on this project and reminded herself to ask the next time she wrote to him, but whatever his reason, she was glad he had. She read the first note again, pausing over the part that made her tear up when she had first read it:

> *"I have never met anyone quite like you in all my life. My heart recognizes you, and I pray yours recognizes me. I sense a greatness in you that calls out to me and asks me if I want to join you for the journey. And my heart says yes."*

As a writer, Karen knew the power of words and knew how much it must have cost for him to write those words to a perfect stranger. It seemed that he was just the sort of person she admired, one who embraced his fear of rejection and did what his heart said to do. In each of the notes, he exposed a bit more of himself to her, through his description of a powerful moment or thought from his day and his reflection on it. The one where he described the dead bird that he found on a Monday morning, broken from having battered itself against the glass window of his classroom in an effort to fly free, was heartbreaking. He saw himself in that bird, wanting a way out of the life he had been living and trying not to lose himself to the illusion he let others see. And he saw her as his reality, though he knew there was much more to learn, and he hoped she would share the learning with him.

So many of his thoughts reflected her own that she wondered if he might be what some people thought of as a soulmate. It had to be incredible after only two meetings to have found so much in common with another human being that the thought was even possible. And yet, what other explanation could there be for it? His words in the notes made her long to spend time with him, listening to him talk about his life, his hopes and dreams, his wishes and desires. She wanted to know him more, and she hoped the notes he had promised to keep writing would help her with that, too.

She read his reply to her note with a smile. He was so formal, so polite, so Old World charming, and she found it sweetly appealing. She had a story to finish, but she promised herself that she would look at them over the weekend while she was at Toni's house. Which reminded her that she needed to book her bus ride. Doing that online took only a few minutes, then she placed her laptop carefully on the other side of the bed, rolled over, and went to sleep.

The next few days passed in a blur. Karen was immersed in her writing, and except for the day she spent driving around Yorkshire with her brother, she worked from early morning until late at night to meet her deadline. She was leaving on Friday morning for London and wouldn't be back until Monday. She didn't want to have to work over the weekend; she wanted to relax and read Peter's notes. He had sent her more since the last time and said he understood about her not responding until the weekend as he himself had work all week.

The bus ride was uneventful, except for the expected delays on the highway, and by the time she arrived at Toni's apartment, she was pleasantly tired. Toni had left the key with the doorman, and she let herself in with a sigh of relief. She could kick off her shoes, put her feet up, and nap until Toni got home. After a call to tell George she had arrived safe and sound, she lay back on the recliner and fell asleep. Toni woke her when she got home with the tempting flavors of Chinese food being reheated. Her stomach rumbled loudly as she sat up, and she followed her nose to the kitchen.

"Hey you!" Toni said, spying her wandering in. "Had a nice nap?"

"Yes, thanks. I needed it. I've been staying up way too late the past few nights, and you know me—I can't travel and sleep." Karen peered into the containers on the counter. "What's for dinner?" she asked.

"Anything you like from these boxes. Help yourself!" Toni handed her a plate and a spoon.

Karen took garlic chicken wings, broccoli, and pork fried rice and sat at the counter next to her friend. They ate in companionable silence, and only when Toni had emptied her plate did she ask about Karen's guest.

"What do you know about him?" she wanted to know.

"Nothing," was Karen's succinct response. "I met him in a pub."

Toni turned surprised eyes to Karen's face. "You were in a pub? By yourself? Whatever possessed you?"

Karen rolled her eyes at her friend. "You make me sound like a recluse! I was in there the night before with..."

Her hesitation did not go unnoticed. "With? Who with?" At her continued silence, Toni's eyes bulged. "With another man?" She sounded positively scandalized, so much so that Karen laughed despite the small, niggling hurt that she suppressed determinedly. Only as she talked with Toni was she fully realizing how closeted she had let herself become—until even her friends thought her a hermit.

"Why is that so hard to believe? Do I have a tree growing out of my face or something? Yes, with another man. I met him in Amsterdam a few months ago. Well, not met, exactly, more like bumped into and nearly knocked over. And then we met again at the British Museum a few weeks ago."

Toni eyed her friend speculatively. "Been keeping secrets from me, eh? So, what's this other chap's name? Is he Dutch? What do you know about him? And how did you end up in a pub with him?"

"He asked me out for a drink," Karen replied and closed her mouth. But she should have known her friend would not relent, and so she found herself telling Toni all she knew about Peter, excluding the writing he had been sending to her. That was still too new, too precious to share with anyone. She laughed when Toni concluded that he must be a homely-looking man as Karen had not indicated he was also a chick magnet.

"He's very handsome, and tall, and blue-eyed," she corrected Toni. "But he's not your average chick magnet. He's much more understated. Maybe it's to do with his job or his personality. He's nowhere near as pushy as Niall!"

"So, you're saying he's a dud!" Toni concluded.

Karen laughed again. "No, silly! Do you know me to be a dud kinda woman? He's just a different kind of man. I'm sure if you were to meet him, you'd see what I mean. He's got an Old World feel about him ... you know what I mean. Charming, courtly, thoughtful." She stopped talking when she realized she was gushing about a man she barely knew and hoped Toni would let it go.

She didn't. "You sound like you're smitten with this Dutchman, missy!" she teased, chuckling. "Now I really want to meet the guy who beat out a chick magnet for your attention!"

Karen held her peace. It wouldn't do to let Toni get started in on the teasing, or it would never end, and the last thing she needed right now was anyone else knowing about what amounted to a schoolgirl crush, albeit a very heavy one, on a twice-met man. She finished her meal and took a glass of wine with her into the living room. She knew her friend was an avid British comedy fan, and there were a set of them about to start. She sat with her feet curled under her and laughed her way through three hours of television before she decided to call it a night. She wanted to re-read Peter's notes and send him a quick one of her own before bed.

"What time do I need to be ready for this party, how shall I dress, and what can I do to help?" she asked as Toni opened the sleeper couch for her.

"The party's at eight, and the dress is club formal, and no, there's nothing for you to do. It's all been taken care of. Does your date know where to come?"

"Yes, I told him." She helped Toni spread the bed, then set her bag on top before following Toni to the linen closet where she chose a towel and washcloth.

"I'm going to take a bath and turn in now," Toni announced. "I'm bushed! Goodnight! Sleep well, sweetie!" She waggled her fingers at Karen as she disappeared into her bedroom.

CHAPTER 7

While Toni bathed, Karen set out her night things and re-read Peter's notes. In one of them, he confessed to daydreaming about her while at work, and remarked on how pleasant an activity that had become for passing the time between classes, or in meetings which were dull. She smiled as she read it and decided to respond to that one.

Dear Peter,

I've had a chance to re-read the notes you sent me, and I wonder why you started to write them at all, and that you could find anything to daydream about me. Poor thing! You must be starving for some mental stimulation, which I am happy to supply! *chuckles* At any rate, your notes are very poignant, and I find they give me a whole lot to think *about. Thank you. I hope you have a good night ... you're probably asleep already. Sweet dreams!*

K

She clicked "Send" and went to have a shower. As soon as her head touched the pillow, she was out like a light and did not wake until she heard rustlings in the kitchen. She rolled over and stretched, wishing she could stay in bed longer. But this was her friend's living room, the stage for tonight's party, and she would need to ensure that it was spotless and free of the appearance of a bedroom. She got up slowly and took her things into Toni's bedroom, then returned to fold the bed back into a couch and fluff the cushions before taking herself off for morning ablutions. Clad in shorts and an old t-shirt, she wandered into the kitchen. Toni was just dishing up scrambled eggs and bacon.

"Oh good, you're up! Let's eat!"

She put the eggs and bacon on the counter where sliced bread, marmalade, and butter already sat, along with two glasses of apple juice. They helped themselves to the feast and listened idly to the sounds of morning.

"So, what are you going to be doing all day till party time?" Karen asked.

"Nothing much. I had the flat cleaned yesterday, and my friend, the caterer, will be bringing the food and such to set up around six. We have all day to loll about and be lazy!" She grinned. "But I do have an idea of how we can spend at least a couple of hours if you're interested!"

Karen cocked her head and asked, "Interested in ...?

"A mani-pedi! I didn't have time to get it done at the salon, and I absolutely cannot be seen tonight with these!"

She stretched her hands out dramatically and showed Karen what looked like perfectly polished nails.

"I don't see a problem," she said honestly.

"There's a real problem," Toni insisted. "It won't match the outfit I'm wearing!" She laughed merrily as Karen rolled her eyes at her. "So, wanna share the mani-pedi with me? We can do each other's nails, just like old times!"

"Sounds fine to me," Karen said. "But right now I feel like another nap. Which means I need to take myself off for a walk to wake up!"

By the time the caterers arrived, Karen had done more than take a walk and was dozing on the couch. The doorbell woke her, and she went to get it, yawning hugely. The man at the door identified himself and was let in with his crew and their burden of food. Karen disappeared, only reappearing with minutes to spare before the first guests began to arrive. She had opted for a silk dress, knee length and clinging to her every curve. Her sandals were white and strappy, her jewelry understated, her makeup barely there. Toni had whistled at her as she walked into the living room, making Karen chuckle in amusement.

When the doorbell rang, she went to get it and stopped in her tracks when Niall filled the opening. He looked wonderful in a fawn gray suit with a white silk dress shirt, open at the collar, and polished gray loafers.

"Hi! Come in!" she said, relieved to find she could admire him without getting sweaty palms and shortness of breath. She would have been unhappy if her responses to him were like those to Peter, whom she had avoided thinking about all day.

Niall stepped inside and inhaled her fragrance, watching Karen watch him without any more than a friendly eye. He knew then that he had no chance with her, despite his having thought about her a lot since their first meeting. She was as alluring as ever, but elusive, and he felt it in her smile, even as she walked ahead of him into the living room. He assumed this was going to be a small party as the space was intimate, which made him wonder how he was going to handle being so near her when she so obviously didn't return his interest. And then he saw a small, curvy woman in a little black dress walk into the room, and his mind shut down. He knew Karen was speaking to him, but he couldn't focus for a second. It felt as though all the air in the room had been sucked out, and he needed to hold his breath until oxygen was restored.

"Niall?" Karen's concerned voice finally penetrated his haze, and he cleared his throat before answering.

"Sorry," he said, but could find nothing to add to explain his lapse in concentration.

Karen studied him for a second, and the small smile she allowed to purse her lips made him cringe. She knew what had happened, and she knew why, and she was highly entertained by it. But she said nothing, merely introduced her friend.

"Toni, meet Niall McLaren. Niall, my friend Antonia Larson."

Karen watched Toni trip over her feet and almost laughed aloud. Her friend was never clumsy, and the stilettos she wore everywhere except in bed were second nature to her. *Tonight will be very interesting,* she thought, watching them try to release each other's hands. She walked away from them, letting them figure out how to deal with what was clearly an immediate and serious attraction. She only hoped Toni knew how to handle the two men vying for her attention because she could clearly see that Rory Stewart wouldn't be the only man hoping to get in Toni's bed tonight. She chuckled as she snagged a deviled egg and poured herself a glass of wine.

Before long, the party was in full swing. Christine, the birthday girl, arrived, no man in tow, and the few other friends Toni had also invited cheered and hugged and kissed her. Rory Stewart was the last to arrive, and one look at his handsome, blond self and she could see why Toni had been interested. But where he was golden and beautiful, Niall was dark and dangerous. Where he was average height, Niall was a giant. Where he was slender, Niall was all hard bulk and muscle. Yeah, Rory wouldn't win this match. He'd be better off trying for the birthday girl, who was giving him the eye anyway.

Before she knew it, it was midnight. All the food and hard liquor had been consumed with only soft drinks and the remnants of the delicious birthday cake remaining. Everyone but Niall, Christine, and Rory was gone, and Christine was about to take her leave. Toni swept into action, knowing who she wanted to stay. Rory never saw it coming.

"Hey, Ror, I'd love it if you would escort Chrissy home for me. It's kinda late, and I'd be worried about her going by herself in a cab."

Karen watched the two friends exchange knowing glances, which Rory missed completely, but Niall caught. She bit her lip to keep from grinning.

"Sure thing, if it's okay with you," Rory replied congenially.

Karen couldn't read him. He hadn't made any move toward Toni all night and had been circumspect in his behavior to all the women, attached and unattached. So, she didn't know if he was angry or happy that he was leaving with the rail-thin brunette, who looked like a pixie with her short, spiky hair and huge eyes. She barely reached his shoulder, but she smiled at him sweetly and hugged Toni.

"It was nice to meet you," she said, shaking hands with Karen and Niall. "Thanks for making my birthday memorable."

Niall smiled at her, and said, "I think we will all have some happy memories from tonight."

Toni let them out while Karen made herself scarce in the bathroom. She wanted to give them time to sort themselves out and make plans without her being there to cramp their style. She had watched the way they seemed to flow together all evening, like two tributaries of the same river. It was obvious to her, if to no one else, that there was something happening between them, and even though she felt a twinge of envy that her friend had hopefully finally found the right man, she was happy for her. Toni's life had been difficult from the beginning, and she deserved a break. And from the very little Karen knew about Niall, Toni would be in good hands.

Walking back into the living room, trying to be as loud as possible so they would hear her, she nevertheless managed to interrupt a tender moment at the door, where Niall had just bent his head to kiss Toni's cheek. It was a lingering kiss, and he raised his head and said something that made Toni smile and blush. She cleared her throat and walked fully into the room. Neither moved, nor seemed to care about what she might have seen, so she ignored the awkward moment.

"I know this isn't my place, Toni, but I'm ready for some zzz's." She chuckled as she said it, knowing Toni would understand.

Her friend laughed. "You'd better go, Niall. This is Karen's bedroom!"

Niall turned to look at Karen, his black eyes twinkling. "It was good to see you again," he said, walking back to grip her hand in both of his. "And I have a feeling we'll be seeing a lot more of each other from now on." His smile was knowing, and oddly grateful, and she smiled back, watching him leave.

When the door closed behind him, the first words from Toni's mouth made her collapse into a heap on the couch, laughing merrily.

"Whew! I'm still shaking, and all he did was kiss my cheek!"

"So, I was right, eh? He's a chick magnet! And he seems to have caught a chick!"

Toni blushed, surprising Karen. "I've never had that kind of reaction to any man, Karen. Never!" She came to sit beside her friend, hugging herself, and then turned to ask, "You don't mind, do you? I mean, you met him first, and it's obvious he likes you."

Karen reached over to hug her friend. "No, I don't mind. Honestly. I'm just envious, but I'll get over it!" She smiled and then added, "But I'm really serious about needing to sleep. You guys party hard!"

"Okay, I'm going to take another long bath and daydream!"

Once Toni was gone, Karen opened the couch bed and sat with her laptop on it, suddenly eager to see what Peter had sent her. She had deliberately not thought about him all day and had forced herself to stay away from the laptop until now. But the need to "see" him was more than she could bear any longer. When she opened her mailbox, there were two messages from him, sent hours ago while the party was in full swing. The first one was more notes for her, and the second was a response to her last note.

Dear K,

> *I hope you won't be offended when I tell you that the reason I began to write to you was partly to get myself out of the rut I've been in for too many years. Having to articulate how I feel about someone to whom I find myself very attracted is a kind of catharsis for me. And it was my hope, even from the first note, that I could share them with you in the hopes of sparking a like interest in me. I'm happy that at least you are not appalled at my temerity.*
> *As to the question of stimulation, you would be surprised at just how much you stimulate me. At any rate, thanks for the permission. I'll make sure to daydream well from now on!*

*Have a lovely weekend, my
new friend,
P*

Karen could picture his face smiling at her as he talked of stimulation, his blue eyes piercing into her brown ones. She fired off a flirty response, knowing he was probably asleep and would not get it until the morning.

Hi P,

As a writer, it's my business to stimulate my audience, and I daresay I've become something of an expert in many forms. Of course, in your case, I'm happy to provide specialist service, if that is your wish. (She inserted a wink, then changed it to a smile).

I've been celebrating at a birthday party, which is why I haven't answered before now. But I shall send suitably serious replies to the notes tomorrow. Until then, sleep well.

K

She sent it, closed the laptop, and went to take a quick shower before falling into bed.

CHAPTER 8

A gray, rainy morning greeted Peter as he woke to walk the dog. He resisted the urge to check his emails until he returned, and after taking a towel to a very wet dog, he went to shower and change into dry clothes before sitting with his laptop and a cup of coffee. Karen's note made him smile widely, and as he sat there sipping the hot brew, he decided it was time to step up the pace. She seemed interested in him and was even flirting with him. He needed to make the next move. After pouring himself a second cup of joe, he re-read the part of her reply that had made his heart and other body parts clench:

"I've always been a sucker for words," she had written, *"especially when they are wielded like a fine blade by a skillful wordsmith. They seduce me, they arouse me, they take my breath away. And if I were to be the happy recipient of the right sort of touch to accompany the words that reach my soul ... well, can you imagine clay in the hands of a master potter?"*

Even now he felt his blood heat as he thought of molding her willing flesh to his pleasure. He began to type. When he was satisfied with his latest note, he saved it and went on to the chores he had to do. The house help had come the day before, so his apartment was clean and his clothes laundered and ironed. He put away the things she had left neatly folded in the laundry room, then tackled the schoolwork he had brought home with him. It took the better part of the day, but by late afternoon, he was all caught up on his grading, had lessons planned for the week, including a test he was to give on Wednesday, and could happily attend to his evening meal, and the time he hoped to spend online.

After dinner, he sat in his favorite arm-chair, his fully charged laptop on his knees, and opened his emails. Karen had answered again. She was returning to Birmingham tomorrow and was spending the day with Toni and one Niall McLaren (he raised his brow at that ... he'd have to ask about him) but would be home later if he cared to talk. Did that mean she wanted him to call her? What would he say if he did? It was one thing to be mildly flirtatious online with an ocean and a screen between you and the recipient of your attentions, but it was an altogether different prospect to speak with that person. It would be almost like being face-to-face.

He sent a reply via email. Being as uncertain as he was, he didn't need Karen to know how much like an untrained schoolboy he felt around her.

Dear K

I'm glad you would like the stimulants I suggested. Who knows? Perhaps someday we'll meet again serendipitously, and we can try them out. I think I could spend most of my days in your delightful company enjoying such pleasing pursuits. In the meantime, emails are lovely. I am imagining your smile as you read my silly musings, and it warms me.

I've written a lot of poetry over the years but had stopped about six years ago. Since meeting you, however, it seems Erato has returned. I've been saving them, looking for a place to publish them, and I'd be grateful if, when you are able, you would give a few of them your expert eye. The comments you have made on the notes tells me I can trust your instincts.

Who is Niall McLaren? I don't believe you've ever mentioned him. I hope you have enjoyed your day out with your friends. Take care.

P

Just before he sent it off, he remembered to ask her if she had wished to speak with him, then he took Scrooge for his evening stroll, enjoying the rain-washed scent of the cool, damp evening breeze. Upon his return, he fed and watered the dog, and resisting the urge to check his emails, he sat at the piano and played out the tension brought on by his desires in the music of some of his favorite composers. It had been ages since he had spent more than a few minutes at the piano, and the exercise brought back happier times when Alijd was full of laughter and desire and love. Chopin and Beethoven and Vivaldi and Mozart all flowed out of him in a river of emotion. He went where his heart went, playing pieces he had memorized from his childhood, pieces that marked some of the milestones of his life.

They had had no children because Alijd had suffered a terrible accident as a young girl and had been unable to carry children. Although he had asked on several occasions, she had refused to adopt, and he had given up six years ago, around the time she had begun to withdraw from him. Now he felt it was too late for him, but he still wished in his secret heart that he could have had at least one child to call his own, one child to love, to live with as the symbol of his love for the woman who would share her body with the baby and with him. He sighed, then started when the clock struck the hour. It was late ... had he been sitting here for two hours playing and remembering?

He went to make himself a cup of tea, cut a slice of the fruit tart he had bought at the shop, and sat by the kitchen window looking out into the endless night. His thoughts went everywhere, but always seemed to come back to the woman across the pond whose sensuous smile and full breasts were forever branded into his mind and heart. He needed to see her again, to make sure he was not merely exaggerating the qualities he thought made her the woman he should pursue. He had never been so often hard and aching in the last ten years as he had been in the last four months, and the almost nightly dreams that washed his body in sweat and pulled his semen from his rock-hard member at least once a week in wanton disrespect for his vaunted self-control shook him to the core of his being.

He did not know this new self. It had never been like this, not even with Alijd. Even now the thought of Karen made his hand shake on the mug he held. The only way he knew to get back some semblance of control was to see her again and to test the depth and truth of this attraction he could not seem to shake off. His phone rang as he sat there, his tea grown cold, and he stirred himself to answer it.

"Hello there, Peter! It's Jannie! How are you?"

Peter smiled at the sound of his cousin's voice. They had grown up together, though she was older by five years than he, and she had lived in Friesland until she married an English country doctor and had moved back to the UK with him. That had been thirty years ago or so, and Peter only saw her now when they came over to visit, or he went to them.

"I'm doing well, thanks, Jannie! How are you and Duncan?"

"Oh, he's busy, as usual, and I'm happily retired now, thank goodness!"

"Well, congratulations to you!" he said, meaning every word.

Jannie's life had been a hard one, especially after both her parents died when she was ten years old, and she had been taken in by a great aunt whose idea of child rearing was medieval at best. She once had told him that the summers she spent with his family were some of the best she ever had, and that she had loved being his older cousin and giving him all the love she never experienced in her own home. Now she had three children of her own, whom she lavished attention on, and who returned her love in equal measure though none lived with her any longer.

"Thanks, love! Now, I can't talk long, as Duncan will be home soon, and I don't want to spoil the surprise. I've sent you an invitation to his sixtieth birthday party, which will be a couple of Fridays from now. I'd like you to be here, Peter. It's been a year since we've last seen you, and I don't know if your summer plans can include us this year as we're going to Scotland to his ancestral castle for a family reunion. I just wanted to let you know it's coming and also to see whether or not you think you can make it to the party."

Peter did not hesitate. Here was his chance to get back to England, to see Karen, to move his plan along. He knew he would be able to take a day from work and make it up when he got back because the scheduler was his friend, and he had not asked for such a favor in more years than he could remember.

"I'll definitely be there, Jannie," he said. "Is this just for family, or may I bring a friend?"

"You have a special lady friend, Peter? At long last?" Jannie sounded delighted, and though Peter wanted to lie to her and let her believe that he was seeing someone, theirs had never been that sort of relationship.

"Well, it's hard to explain," he said. "For now, let's just say I'd like her to be. Maybe by the time I get there, she will be. At least you'll get to meet her, and we can talk further."

"Well, please do bring her along, then. I'd love to meet the woman who can make my reclusive cousin sound so uncertain!"

She chuckled, and Peter felt a warm glow spreading through him. Jannie reminded him of that past he had long forgotten, when he was part of a warm and loving family, where she had been more doting big sister than cousin. He smiled at her enthusiastic response and tried to caution her.

"She might refuse my invitation," he protested, laughing.

"Oh, I very much doubt that, Peter. I know you too well. You are a very good judge of character, and if you're that interested, she must be, too, or you wouldn't bother!"

"I suppose you're right, at that," he replied.

"I'm glad you'll come, love, even if you bring only yourself. It will be lovely to see you! I'd better go now; I hear Duncan coming in. Good night, dear."

"Good night, Jannie."

Peter went to retrieve his mug, emptied and washed it, and poured himself a large Drambuie, which he took upstairs with him. Settling into bed, he checked his emails at last and found himself strangely elated when he found two messages from Karen. He read them slowly, sipping his drink. In the first one, she agreed to read his poetry, saying she enjoyed his writings, both those meant for her alone and those about the things he had been thinking of during his day. He was flattered by her praise, which was fulsome, and he sensed that she was not merely stroking his ego, but that she sincerely meant the things she said.

Alijd had not ever taken an interest in his writing, finding it "a frivolous and useless waste of time." She had not shared his love of music, and in the later years, he had stopped playing while she was in the house, which meant hardly ever playing, because she complained it was too loud. He had even stopped playing the records and CDs he collected of music through the years by his favorite artists and bands. Shaking his head to clear it of the unhappy memories, he read Karen's second e-mail:

Dear P,

While I'm not as accomplished a poet as you are, I thought you might appreciate this one that I wrote after the party. Please let me know what you think of it, okay?

Serendipity
One chance meeting

stirred something deep,

swelled something pure,

drew something sweet

from his soul's core.

One chance meeting

wrought him the hope,

let him adore,

brought up the dream

from his soul's core.

I was thinking about the way you and I met, and this poem came to me. It's about Niall, but it could just as easily be about either of us. I went back to the pub where we had supper and met him there the next evening. He sat at my table, and we got to talking. He was interested in me and gave me a number where I could reach him. When Toni invited me to her party, she said I could bring a friend, so I asked him. And when he arrived, I could tell at once that they were deeply affected by each other, and I think it's pretty clear, after today, that Niall and I will only be friends, which is fine by me, and by him, I'm sure. And I'm happy for Toni. She deserves to be wanted and (hopefully) loved by someone strong like Niall. Perhaps someday you can meet them.

I'd best be off now. I have an early bus to catch. Sleep well, and sweet dreams!

K

Peter swallowed the rest of his drink as much to calm his nerves as to soothe his heart. There had been another man since they met. That he was obviously not in the picture did not make Peter feel any better about the chance that he might have lost her before he had even gotten her. He supposed he should be grateful her friend Toni and Niall had hit it off, but even that knowledge, and the fact that she seemed to be perfectly happy with the arrangement, could not stop the spurt of irrational jealousy from spiking his blood. Now more than ever, he needed to see her before he lost himself completely to a stranger.

He typed a terse response, unable to flirt with her as before, for fear if he continued to write he would let her see how affected he was by the revelation of a former rival for her affections. She could not know how he felt until he could look her in the eye and gauge her own feelings for him. Words without physical contact could be misconstrued, he knew. He told her the poem was thoughtful and showed the surprise of the speaker nicely, and that he liked the patterns she used in it. He said he would call her the next day in the evening after work as he had something to ask her. Then he wished her a good night and a safe journey back to Birmingham and signed off.

He wrote two notes afterward. The first was as short as his email had been and painfully honest. He would not hide his feelings from her, but he knew that this note was not one he would share with her until he knew where they stood. The second, which he saved and sent with the week's set, shared his reminiscences after his phone conversation with Jannie. Talking about Jannie soothed him, and it set the scene for his invitation the next day, which he had decided he wanted to make on the phone. He needed to hear her voice, to gauge her feelings, to read the pauses, the breaths, the spaces between her words.

CHAPTER 9

While Peter tossed and turned, unable to sleep, Karen was packing and getting ready to leave for home. Toni was still asleep when she stole quietly out of the apartment at four in the morning. She had left her friend a note, and as she rode in the cab to the bus station, she found herself smiling again at the way life worked. Niall had returned yesterday morning, his usual cheerful self, and invited them both out for the day. His friends were having a barbecue, and they lived two hours away, so he thought a nice ride in the country would be a pleasant way to spend a Sunday with his two favorite ladies. Karen smiled at the memory. She was glad she felt not even a twinge of hurt that he had chosen Toni over her because she would not have been able to return the heated regard he often directed toward her friend.

She had not had time to read her emails before leaving, so she took the time to check them while she waited to board the bus. Peter's message was shorter than usual, and he had sent a set of notes for the week. Karen felt a vague misgiving, though nothing in the message gave her cause to feel that anything was wrong. She wondered what he had to ask her that needed him to speak with her directly. She had a whole day now to anticipate his call and to prepare herself to hear his voice again. She read his notes next, trying to see if anything in them would give her a reason to worry that things were not right, but nothing felt wrong in them either. She fretted about it the whole way home and all day. By the time her phone rang after nine in the evening, she was a mass of nerves.

"This is Karen. How may I help you?"

"Good evening, Karen. It's Peter."

His voice stroked her, almost like a physical touch, and she inhaled deeply before answering.

"Hi, Peter. How are you?"

"I'm well, thank you, Karen. I hope you are, too?"

"Yes, thanks, I am."

There was definitely something wrong, but nothing he had said so far made it plain. Karen decided to take the bull by the horns.

"Is something wrong, Peter?" she asked quietly and waited for his answer.

He paused, then cleared his throat and said, "Not really, no."

Which told her nothing, being the most inconclusive answer in the world. She bit back a sharp retort and waited, hoping he wouldn't make her wait too much longer before he relieved the growing tension between them. He didn't.

"I've been wanting to hear your voice again, actually, and to see you. And another rather serendipitous—that seems to be our word, doesn't it?—event might make that possible if you're available." He sounded conflicted, as though he wanted something he didn't think he would get from her.

She clenched the fist not holding the phone. "And what is that?"

"My cousin Jannie is hosting a sixtieth birthday party for her husband in two weeks and has invited me to attend. I've accepted, and she has said I may bring a friend. Would you care to join me?"

Karen's heart leapt, but she managed to keep her voice even. "Where is this party being held?"

"Jannie and Duncan live in Woodstock," he said. "It's very pretty country thereabouts, and if you're into day tripping, there's a lot of scenic touring to be done as well. Plus, it's close to Oxford and so on."

"Peter, I'd love to go with you. You don't have to sell me on it, okay?" Karen chuckled at him. He was clearly nervous, and she wanted to put him at ease, even though his nervousness eased her own mind. "Do I have to pack for more than an overnight stay?"

"Yes. We'll be arriving on Friday a little before the party and staying till Sunday." He paused, then added, "You'll like my cousin. She was like a big sister to me when we were younger."

"When shall I be ready?" she wanted to know next.

"I'd like to set off by early afternoon if you don't mind. Three o'clock would be good. It'll give us time to breathe before the party starts."

"I assume I'll be staying in a hotel?" Karen's tone was matter-of-fact.

"I'll let you know about that the next time we speak, I promise, but I shouldn't think so." He cleared his throat again, then said, "I'm glad you're coming with me. I've been wanting to break bread with you again and to look into your lovely brown eyes as we talk of this and that."

Karen ducked her head and blushed, as though he were sitting next to her and could see her. "I've found that absence makes the memory go soft, haven't you?" She tried to pass off the attraction with a joke.

"No, I can't say I have," he disagreed softly, his voice a low seduction in her ear. "Your brown eyes have a ring of burnished gold around the very dark center. There's no way to forget that. Nor would I wish to. I find them stimulating all by themselves."

Karen felt her cheeks warming again and was happy he was not there to see her schoolgirl reactions. She chuckled to hide her true feelings.

"No more so than your blue eyes that can't decide if they're more blue than grey," she said.

He chuckled softly. "I've been told that before. They do seem to change color sometimes," he admitted, "but I'm not usually the one who notices it."

A small, comfortable silence ensued before Peter ended the call. "I need to go now. I have to get up early in the morning. Lots to do before I go to work. Have a pleasant week!"

"Thanks, Peter. You too! Good night!"

"Good night, *liefje*." Karen heard the endearment and knew what it meant (thank you, Betty Neels!). She hugged it to her heart as she hung up.

The next two weeks seemed to fly by as Karen met her deadlines, hung out with Toni for a night out so they could catch up—she and Niall had hit it off, and Karen was happy for her friend's good fortune—and by the time Peter called her to say she would be staying with him at his cousin's, she was in a fine state of anticipation mixed with some healthy trepidation. He had said the dress would be formal befitting his cousin's husband's status in the community and involvement in public life. She packed and repacked her weekender, worrying over what to wear for the party itself, and what to wear while there so as not to embarrass herself or Peter. Finally, she settled on a little black dress—when was that ever *not* a success?—a sundress for Saturday, and jeans and a t-shirt for Sunday. She finished packing and went to sleep finally after reading the notes he had sent her a few hours earlier.

"You never told me you had a man, baby girl," George commented next morning at breakfast when she told him her plans, a big grin splitting his face. "Been holding out on me, eh?"

Karen smiled. "First of all, I'm not a baby," she said, rolling her eyes at the chuckle that escaped him, "and second, I don't have a man, as you put it. Peter is just a friend."

"Is he male?" George asked innocently. Snatching the roll she threw at him out of the air, he opined, "Then he is your man!" He chuckled when she stuck her tongue out at him. "Especially as you'll be spending the weekend with him!" he concluded triumphantly.

"I'm not spending the weekend with him, George! Jeez! His cousin has invited me to spend the weekend in her home. Just because he's going to be there too doesn't mean I'm spending it with him! You're impossible!" she huffed good-naturedly. "It's a wonder you're not demanding to meet him before he takes me away for a weekend of debauchery."

"There's to be debauchery, then?" he teased, raising an amused brow.

Karen laughed, and he joined her. She loved it that she had someone she could be herself with, someone who loved her and cared about her happiness. George never judged her, even when she was busy condemning herself.

"I'll introduce you when he comes to pick me up," she promised. "At least that way, you'll know what he looks like if I disappear or come back with my reputation in ruins!"

They shared another laugh and finished their meal. When Peter rang the doorbell at three o'clock precisely, Karen was rolling her case down the stairs. George heard the loud thumping as he came out of the sitting room to answer the door and came to take it from her.

"I'll get the door," she said, relinquishing her hold on the case and hurrying to let Peter in.

He was backlit by the afternoon sun, and she blinked to get his face into focus. He was smiling as she invited him in, and when the door was closed, she made the introductions.

"Peter, meet my brother George Mullings. George, my friend, Peter van der Meulen."

Peter and George shook hands, and Peter said, "A pleasure to meet you!" before he took the luggage with him out to the car.

George and Karen followed, and as Peter opened the passenger door for her, George hugged her and said as he kissed her cheek, "Don't do anything I wouldn't do!"

Peter's grin lit up his face, though he said nothing in response, as Karen smacked her brother in the arm, laughing.

"That means I have a lot of freedom, then!" she quipped and smirked at him as she waved goodbye.

"Hello, petal!" Peter's voice broke into her amused thoughts as they turned onto the main drag. Karen looked questioningly at him.

"Petal?" she asked.

His eyes briefly took in the daisy-decorated top she wore above a pair of loose-fitting stone-washed jeans. Karen smiled at the nickname and wondered what they would talk about for the next two hours. Peter answered her unspoken question because he seemed to be well-versed in the areas they drove through and kept up a gentle running commentary that made the journey seem to go by quickly. When they were close to Woodstock, he turned to look briefly at her before saying, his eyes once again on the road, "I'm very pleased that you agreed to be my date, Karen. I know you'll like Jannie. She's a lovely woman."

She could hear the affection for his cousin in his voice. "And Duncan? Will I like him, too?" she asked.

"Duncan is a bit reserved with strangers, but he'll be hospitable, especially as the occasion is in his honor. And no doubt he'll be more open than usual because I've brought a woman with me."

She looked at him, puzzled, and it occurred to her that she really knew very little about this man whom she had been fantasizing about almost from the moment she had bumped into him in Amsterdam.

"I've been a widower for the last four years," he explained, his voice expressionless.

"Oh, I'm so sorry!" she exclaimed, shocked and embarrassed. Here she had been salivating over a man who was clearly still mourning his dead wife.

"No, that's all right. Alijd and I were essentially estranged for years before she died." His tone remained completely without feeling, as though he were discussing the weather. Karen turned to look at him properly, wishing she could see his face, see his eyes, to see if he was really as unaffected as he appeared to be. There were things she wanted to ask, but she bit her tongue, waiting for him to offer.

"She had been diagnosed with cancer after we had been married for ten years, and following the treatments, she went into remission. But then, five years ago, it returned, more aggressive than usual, and within a year, she was dead."

"I'm sorry, Peter. Death is never pleasant, even when it is expected."

Karen didn't know what else to say because she had no idea how he felt about anything he had told her. And she noted he had said nothing about why he and his wife had been estranged. He didn't seem to be the kind of man who would have been the cause of that estrangement, but as she knew even less about his wife than she knew about him, she was going entirely on faith.

Evidently, he was done talking because the last few minutes of the journey were made in silence, and when he turned onto his cousin's driveway, Karen wondered when, if ever, they would return to the conversation they had left on the highway. He came around to help her out, then retrieved their luggage from the trunk. She followed him to the front door, which opened before she could knock, as though his cousin had been looking out for them.

"Hello there!" a tall, angular woman greeted them, a smile of welcome on her pretty face. "You must be Karen," she said, smiling and extending her hand.

"It's lovely to meet you," Karen said, shaking her hand and letting herself be led into a warm living room. Peter followed them, and his cousin waited until he had put down the luggage before hugging him warmly.

"How are you, Peter?" Jannie asked, pulling away from his arms to look him over. "It's so good to see you! At least you don't look so gaunt anymore!" She reached over to kiss his cheek again and then said, "Come through. I'm sure you'd like a cup of tea before you go up to change."

She led them into her big country kitchen, and they sat around the woodblock table and sipped tea while she brought her cousin up to date on the party plans. Duncan would be home in a few minutes and would be getting ready for a party she had told him they had been invited to. It was to be a formal affair, and as he never usually remembered what events he had been invited to, and she was always the one to organize the attendance at such functions, Duncan would not be at all suspicious. Since he never remembered his birthday either, the surprise would be complete. She asked Peter to move his car to the side, where Duncan would not see it readily, and while he did that, she showed Karen to her room.

"Duncan won't get back downstairs till around 6:15, so you have a bit of time to freshen up. You and Peter will share a bathroom. I hope you don't mind."

Jannie was solicitous, but Karen felt an undercurrent of interest in her and Peter's relationship that she did not know how to satisfy.

"No, that won't be a problem at all. Thank you for agreeing to put me up," she replied, feeling oddly embarrassed.

"I'll see you downstairs, then," Jannie said and went away.

Karen unpacked her dress and hung it up, glad it was the sort of material that did not wrinkle easily. By the time she was ready to slip it on, the few creases would have smoothed themselves out. Unpacking the rest of her things quickly, she was about to go to the bathroom to wash her face when a knock sounded on her door. It was Peter, wanting to know if she was all right, and informing her that he would be coming to escort her downstairs at about 6:10 or so.

"I'm just on the other side of the bathroom if you need anything, okay?"

Karen smiled her thanks. "Is it okay if I go first?" she asked, indicating the bathroom.

"Yes, of course," he replied and took himself off.

CHAPTER 10

H alf an hour later, her hair swept up off her shoulders, her stockinged legs encased in high-heeled black sandals, Karen surveyed her reflection in the full-length, free-standing mirror. Her face was warmly made up, the colors subtle, but she saw the flush in her cheeks that had nothing to do with rouge and everything to do with the man in the bedroom next to hers. She berated herself for being worried about what he might think of her appearance, but when she opened her door at his knock and saw the look in his eyes, she grew warm with emotion.

"You look very lovely, Karen!" he said, his voice hoarse as though he were developing a cold. His eyes took in her neck and shoulders, the latter left bare by the off-the-shoulder cut of the dress, which clung to her breasts like a second skin, flaring out gently from the waist to tease him.

"Thank you!" she answered, then let her eyes roam his person.

His suit was dark gray, the shirt he wore a blue to match the eyes he kept trained on her. He had shaved again, and his cheeks were smooth and cool, his lips slightly parted as though he were on the verge of speech. He smelled of some clean, masculine fragrance, and underneath it all was that subtle flavor that was him. Her mouth watered, and she swallowed, placing her hand in the crook of his arm. Her whole body reacted to the feel of his muscle under the suit jacket, and she inhaled deeply to calm her quaking nerves.

"Let's go down the back stairs to the kitchen, so we won't run the chance of bumping into Duncan before Jannie can spring the surprise," he suggested and led her along the passage to the opposite end of the hall and down into the kitchen. The room seemed crowded, though when she counted, there were only nine other people in it. She was introduced as Peter's friend, then Jannie went to get her husband, who could be heard whistling as he came down the stairs.

Duncan's shock when he walked into the kitchen to shouts of "Surprise!" was almost comical. And as they sang him the birthday song, he went a bright red and smiled in an I'd-rather-be-dead-than-here sort of way. But he put on a game face, and by the time the party was in full swing, he seemed much more relaxed. These people were his family and close friends, so Karen assumed it was just his innate reservedness that had made him react as he had before. When Peter took her over to be introduced, after handing Jannie the bottle she had not noticed until then that he had been holding, Duncan's eyes grew sharp with speculation.

"Duncan, many happy returns!" Peter said, shaking his hand. "I'd like you to meet a friend of mine," he continued, pulling her forward gently. "This is Karen Mullings. Karen, my cousin Duncan."

Duncan's smile was genuinely delighted as he shook hands with her, though his eyes went almost immediately back to Peter's face.

"How did you meet?" he asked.

"We bumped into each other in Amsterdam a few months ago, literally," Peter explained with a smile at Karen.

She returned the smile, adding, "More accurately, I bumped into him! And then we met again in London recently."

"Well, I'm very glad to meet you, Karen," Duncan said, finally relinquishing her hand. He winked at her, surprising her, given his apparent reticence before. She smiled at him and noted that he looked his Dutch in-law over with an amused eye.

Karen was introduced to each partygoer, including the two latecomers whose train had been delayed. They were all of an age, older than she was, talented and beautiful and warm people, and they all got along remarkably well for having so little time to spend together each year. She knew they were watching her and wondering who she was to Peter, and she admitted to herself that that was no more than she was thinking as well.

Jannie sat them across from each other at the table, an incredibly impressive thing that took up almost all the space in what she called the great room, which was the dining room and living room together with the door between them slid open to allow for just such an occasion. Peter looked his fill at the beautiful woman who had chosen to partner him for this affair. She was an exotic bloom among the pale lilies with her copper-colored skin and delicious curves. Even her lips, wrapped just now around the spoon for her soup, were a distracting arc of flesh driving him crazy. He forced himself to attend to what his neighbors were asking him, to brush off their commiserations at the loss of Alijd—"It's been four years!" he explained quietly to the one on his right—and to listen to their stories of life since the last time he had seen them.

Under normal circumstances, he would have been happy to listen, but nothing about these circumstances was normal, and his libido had not stopped kicking him in the groin since he had seen her inside her brother's house, her arms bare, her breasts a temptation he fought to resist gazing at. Now, despite the table between them, and the conversation and laughter around him, the assault was harder than ever, and his powers of concentration were being sorely tested. He prayed silently that dinner would soon be over, and they could all retire to the back patio for some much-needed fresh air. He would need it in great gulps if he was to avoid making an absolute ass of himself with her.

He caught Duncan's eye and saw the knowing twinkle in it with a sense of despair, mixed inexplicably with relief. He didn't need anyone else knowing how deeply under Karen's spell he already was before he allowed himself to admit it, yet there was a kind of satisfaction in knowing that what he was feeling was real enough that a discerning and caring eye could see it. He looked away and caught her just as she smiled at something said to her by Jack Talbot, another physician and friend. Her lips curled sensually, her teeth gleamed through, and he licked his own lips in sudden thirst. He wanted to feel those lips under his, to spear that mouth with his hungry tongue, to …

"Don't you agree, Peter?" Jannie's voice pierced the haze of increasing lust that he had let himself sink into, and he reddened at the feeling of all eyes on him.

"Sorry, cuz, I was woolgathering. What did you say?" He made the best of a bad situation, knowing only Duncan may have had some inkling of the reason for his distraction.

"I was saying that it's been a while since we've had a family reunion, and thought we might pull it off this summer. Don't you agree? We've already decided that the venue will be Duncan's family castle in Scotland, but we'll need to finalize dates. What do you think?"

"It's a splendid idea, my dear," he said approvingly, avoiding Karen's interested gaze. "Whatever you decide, I'll do my best to fit it into my very packed schedule!"

His sardonic tone was meant to highlight the irony of his words, and everyone enjoyed a hearty laugh at his expense. Although it bothered him to realize that his family and friends knew the depth of his deprivation, at least it took their minds off the reason he had been woolgathering and gave him a chance to regain control.

By the time Jannie was serving dessert, Peter was calm enough to sit next to Duncan and carry on a sensible conversation about his cousin's latest philanthropic project. But his hope of avoiding any mention of his newfound relationship was dashed when Duncan leaned toward him.

"So, are you going to tell me about the delectable Miss Mullings? Or do I have to ask her myself?"

Peter sighed, not sure how to answer Duncan, and not too thrilled that his cousin was paying such close attention to his woman. *His* woman. The thought shuddered through him, making him catch his breath. He desperately wanted her to be his, but a couple of bland dates in the company of masses of people would provide him nothing in the way of opportunities to make her so. And they still had much to say to each other.

"I'd sooner you kept your opinions as to her delights to yourself, if you don't mind!" he said sharply, completely shocking himself, and amusing Duncan to no end. His cousin burst into delighted laughter, drawing Jannie's eyes to them.

"I'm sorry, my friend! I'll curtail my observations to those of a clinical nature!" Duncan finally managed, still chuckling. "Now, tell me exactly how she came to bump into you, and how you met again, and why you are still denying yourself the pleasure of her ... er, charms?"

Peter saw the amusement still in his cousin's eye and bit back another sharp retort. He wasn't a schoolboy, and Duncan had no interest in Karen apart from the one all men have in a beautiful woman as an object of admiration.

"What makes you think I am denying myself anything?" he demanded instead.

"I've been keeping an eye on the pair of you all evening, and it's clear to me that the two of you are still dancing around each other. What's more, my dear fellow, it's equally obvious that she has you spun around, and you don't know your head from your tail with her. I don't believe I've ever seen you in such a lather. You're like a racehorse, chomping at the bit and rearing to go!"

"What are we talking about?" Jannie's voice interrupted, forestalling Peter's reply.

"Your cousin's faltering love life, my dear!" He kissed his wife's hand where she had it on his shoulder, and the easy familiarity and intimacy between them pierced Peter to the heart. He wanted that. He needed that ... with Karen.

"She is a lovely thing, isn't she, Duncan? Just what the doctor ordered for my stick-in-the-mud cousin to get him out of the doldrums and put some pep in his step!"

Jannie offered her opinion with a sweet smile to take the sting out of her words, but Peter knew she was serious. After four years without a woman, during which Jannie had encouraged and cajoled and bullied and begged him to take back his life, Karen was the first sign any of them had that he might be making a new start. If they only knew exactly how much she had moved him from ground zero, they'd be shocked, but he also knew they'd be cheering him on vigorously.

"Thank you for allowing me to invite her," he said, "as I needed to find a way to see her again, and this was the perfect chance."

"Anything to oblige, love! Wouldn't it be lovely if she were to come to the family reunion as somewhat more than just a friend?"

Jannie sounded so hopeful that Peter had to smile. *My cousin is a true romantic, one of a dying breed,* he thought.

"It would," he agreed.

"I'll just go put some music on before everyone leaves and serve up coffee and liqueurs," Jannie said, leaning down to kiss her husband's cheek. "Oh, and thank you for the Beerenburg, by the way! You are a dear!" She turned and walked away with a smile.

Peter's eyes followed her, as did her husband's, and noted that Karen joined her. Peter turned to watch Duncan's face soften with love and his eyes gleam with desire for the woman he had been married to now for thirty-one years. They had married young, Jannie being seven years Duncan's junior, and it seemed to Peter that their love had only grown over time. He swallowed the ball of hurt that tried to surface and, excusing himself, went to walk in the dimly lit garden. He was suddenly no longer in the mood to discuss the possibility that he might have found someone to make him feel human again. He needed some space to release the pain he had bottled up inside him for all these years, and he could well do without an audience.

A sound made him turn his head, and Karen stood behind him with a glass in her hand.

"Jannie said you like this," she said, coming toward him and offering him the drink. "It's Drambuie."

Peter smiled and took the glass, resisting the urge to take her hand and pull her into him.

"Thank you," he said instead and took a deep swallow, savoring the mellow flavor on his tongue.

"Are you having a good time?" he asked, setting the drink on the waist-high stone wall that separated Jannie's garden from the wooded lot behind it.

"Yes, I am," she answered, sliding her eyes away from his. "Your family is very special." She chuckled.

"Care to share the joke?"

"I was just thinking how reserved Duncan appeared to be when we first met, yet now he seems to be quite relaxed. I guess he sees that

I'm harmless," she concluded with another husky chuckle.

"I wouldn't say that," he demurred, turning fully to face her and reaching for her, finally unable to resist the lure of her presence.

Karen felt the touch of his hands on her bare shoulders like electricity zapping through her body. It shook her to her core, and she raised her face to him.

"I have wanted to kiss you since the first time I saw you," Peter said, his gaze holding hers. "Please don't say no."

Karen stared bemusedly at him as he lowered his mouth to taste her. His blue eyes never left her brown ones as he opened his mouth over hers. His breath was hot and smelled of the whiskey he had been drinking. It was sweet, and she felt herself trembling as he tasted her lips, one at a time, slowly, achingly, and it occurred to her that he was waiting for her to invite him in, to open the way for him to take her mouth in a kiss she knew she had wanted for almost as long as he had. She sighed and let him in.

Peter felt the gust of her breath on his lips when she opened for him, and his blood roared in his ears. He had to remind himself that he was a middle-aged man who had been married for twenty years and knew how to kiss a woman without mauling her. He wanted to whimper and roar at the same time, so great was the emotion welling in his chest. He settled his mouth over hers and thrust his tongue inside, catching hers and suckling it. She moaned, and his blood heated more. He kissed her deeply, wildly, hungrily, holding her face in his hands to draw her as close to him as he could. She tasted like nectar, and he drugged himself on her kisses, glorying in the feel of her mouth, in the way she kissed him back as though she were as ravenous for him as he was for her.

Their bodies fused together in an aching need for more, and Peter pulled himself away from her with a Herculean effort, knowing if he let himself continue to feast on her, he would embarrass them both. He knew she must have felt the clear evidence of his desire for more than the taste of her lips when he had dragged her willing body into his own, and he knew equally well they could not yet go where his rampant flesh wanted them to.

"Much as I would like to continue to indulge myself, I think you had best go back to the party before you are missed, *liefje*." He forced the words between lips throbbing with the urgent need to devour her and let her go. "I'll come in later, in case Jannie asks."

"All right. I'll tell her," Karen said, shaking with suppressed desire and tingling with unfulfilled need, and turned back to the house.

Peter watched her walk away from him and groaned. He knew it would be another long night, and from the way his body was clenched, he'd need relief. He wished he could take his relief with the woman who turned back just then to smile at him as though she knew exactly what he was thinking and wished it too.

CHAPTER 11

K aren listened distractedly to Jannie rambling on about the people who had been such lively company at the party, hearing with only half an ear the things she said about them. She must have hidden her distraction well because Jannie kept right on talking until her husband came in with Peter. She broke off in mid-sentence to accept the kiss Duncan planted on her while Peter looked at Karen unblinkingly.

"I was just telling Karen about the walking marathon we did last year with Jack and the other chaps. She said she'd be interested in doing it with us this year. Didn't you, Karen?"

Karen fought to keep her cheeks from flushing as she realized Jannie was no fool and had known she was not being attentive. Never one to run from a challenge, Karen looked her hostess square in the eye.

"I'm sorry, I must have missed that part, Jannie," she admitted. "I'm not sure I have the stamina to do a marathon, even if it is a walking one!" She gave herself full marks for how she handled her response, adding, for extra points, "Besides, I live in Birmingham for the moment, so it wouldn't be too practical for me to join in a marathon all the way down here, would it?"

"Oh, but you could come and visit on the weekends to train with us and get to know the course, love," Jannie rebutted.

"It's a lovely course," Duncan said, clearly aiding and abetting his wife, "and the people hereabouts are very pleasant company. And I daresay Peter might even find himself available for a visit every now and again too, if you were here!"

Karen stole a glance at Peter and was surprised to find him smiling indulgently at his cousin. She decided that ribbing was all right if he wasn't bothered by it, so she chuckled in her turn.

"You give me too much credit, Duncan! I'm sure Peter has many other things he had rather be doing than dance attendance, even fleetingly, on a wannabe walking marathoner!" It sounded like she was fishing for a compliment, and Karen was embarrassed as soon as the words left her mouth. She stopped speaking abruptly, then spoke again before anyone could respond.

"Anyway, it's been a pretty long day for me. I'll turn in now. Thank you for dinner, Jannie, and happy birthday, Duncan!"

She turned and fled up the back stairs, disappearing into her room as quickly as she could. Her cheeks were red with the depth of her embarrassment, and she fervently hoped that by the time she emerged from her room in the morning, no one would recall the statement, or her hasty retreat. She changed slowly, and as she brushed her teeth, washed her face, and applied a night cream, she wondered what had been said after her abrupt departure from the kitchen. They all probably found her a great diversion, she fumed, because she didn't think before she spoke. Making her way back to her room, she closed the connecting bathroom door and locked it, then rubbed a bit of lotion on her hands before turning down her bed and sitting on the edge.

She didn't think Peter would be sending her any emails this weekend, and she was loathe to be disappointed if she checked and he hadn't. Besides, there hadn't been time today, unless he had sent them on his way over from Leeuwarden. She chose instead to finish the book she had been reading and was still bright-eyed and bushy-tailed when Peter finally made it into the bathroom himself. She could hear water running and found herself blushing faintly at the intimacy of the situation, suddenly happy that he had not been privy to her own nighttime rituals in the bathroom. And yet she found she wanted to be able to share the intimacy to its fullest measure.

She was about to switch off the light when she heard a knock on her side of the bathroom door. She blinked, not sure she had heard right, but then she heard it again. Snatching up her dressing gown, she went to see what he wanted, glancing at the clock as she opened the door. It was well past midnight.

"I saw the light on under the door and hoped you hadn't fallen asleep with it on," he began. Karen waited, looking inquiringly at him. "I hope you weren't upset with Duncan earlier," he went on. "I just wanted to check that you were all right."

Karen smiled. "I'm fine, Peter, though I do have to admit to feeling a bit embarrassed at the end."

He didn't answer. He was staring at her, and she remembered belatedly that her night attire was short—a thin baby blue knee-length night-gown covered by a short, thin dressing gown, both soft cotton. Her hand went self-consciously to her throat, pulling the lapels of the dressing gown together and resisting the blush that was beginning to warm her cheeks. She could feel the tension rising between them, thick, hot, over-whelming, and she spoke to break it and hopefully bring some semblance of common sense back to the situation.

"Thanks for worrying, Peter, but I'm really all right. I'll see you in the morning, okay?"

Still, he didn't answer, and when she looked into his face again, his blue eyes were blazing, and yet so dark they were almost purple. He reached for her and pulled her sharply against his chest, holding her arms to keep her where he wanted her. She couldn't move, couldn't struggle, couldn't free herself even if she wanted to.

"I also came for a goodnight kiss," he said, star-tling her. Before she could speak, he put a finger to her lips and explained, "I'm not the sort of man who ravages women. I don't lose control, ever. But since the moment you bumped into me, I have been anything but the stick-in-the-mud Jannie knows me to be. You're in my head sleeping and waking. I dream of you, and when I am awake, I cannot stem the thoughts that rush through my mind. And now that I have finally had the chance to taste you, I want more."

Karen watched him move to hold her at arm's length so he could take in her whole body, and as his eyes moved heatedly from her face down her chest to her knees, lingering for a while on the place where hip met thigh, she felt herself growing warmer and beginning to tremble. He did not let her go, and when she could not bear his scrutiny a second longer, she pulled her arms away from his hard hands.

"And I'm not the sort of woman who entertains men in her bedroom after hours in her night wear. But it seems my control has also been shot by..." She hesitated, and Peter pounced on it.

"By?" He waited, now taking in her lips and her eyes.

"By my thoughts of you," she said in a small voice.

He inhaled deeply and pulled her back to his body, this time wrapping his arms around her. She returned the favor, draping her arms around his waist.

"Then perhaps we need to lose control together," he suggested in a low, seductive tone. "It may be the only way to keep our sanity." His breath warmed her lips when he asked, "What do you say?"

Karen smiled in answer and raised herself on tiptoes to catch his mouth with hers. He groaned and took over the kiss, teasing her with sexy nips on each lip followed by arousing sucking before he took her whole mouth again, ravaging it, devouring her. She moaned and relaxed completely against him, and he leaned against the door and pulled her into his hardening body, never leaving the sweetness of her mouth. They lost themselves in the tangling of tongues and the heat of hungry bodies pressed against each other. When she came to her senses and dragged her mouth away from his, Peter growled, making her smile.

"That was some kiss goodnight, *Mijnheer van der Meulen*!" she quipped. She was breathing as hard as he was, holding on to him now to keep her knees from buckling.

"Which you ended too soon, *Juffrouw Mullings*!" he complained, pulling her back to his mouth to eat at her again. "I could kiss you all night," he whispered, finally releasing her while letting her feel how true his statement was in the hardness he pressed against her.

Karen inhaled deeply, resisting the urge to rub herself against him. She knew that they would get there eventually because he had wakened the hunger she had kept submerged for all this time with his words, his boldness, and the kisses that she could still feel and taste, and she was suddenly impatient. But she would not give in to lust. Not without being sure the feelings she was harboring for him were fully returned. She had given her body to enough other men who didn't care about her as a person, but merely as a hole for them to jack off in, to know she was not satisfied with sex alone, that she wanted a heart connection with it. And she sensed that with this man, finally, she might have hit the jackpot. But it would be up to him to prove that to her before she let the passion she now struggled with rise fully to the surface.

"Goodnight, Peter," she said, taking another deep breath. "Thank you for checking up on me." She smiled at the glint in his eyes. "What time is breakfast?"

"It's whenever you wake up, *liefje*," he answered, his eyes straying again to her kiss-swollen mouth. "Jannie doesn't stand on ceremony with family."

Before she could respond, he bent his head and kissed her again, an achingly sweet and tender kiss, and she could tell from the way he held her that he was struggling to keep from deepening it.

"*Heerlijk!*" he said, raising his head reluctantly.

"No fair!" she answered, raising accusing eyes to his face. "I don't know much Dutch!"

Peter smiled, and the dimple in his cheek teased her. She reached up without thinking and touched a finger to it, and he hissed and grabbed her hand, bringing it to his mouth.

"It's what you say about food that tastes good," he explained, kissing her knuckles. "Or about the lips of someone you want to keep kissing."

Karen could not stem the rush of color to her cheeks at his words and the feel of his mouth on her skin. Her hand trembled in his, and he smiled again.

"*Goedenacht, liefje,*" he whispered. "Sweet dreams." Another gentle kiss on her lips and he retreated to his side of the bathroom door, leaving her to close and lock it again and drift back to bed.

Peter lay in the dark room staring at the LED time display on the clock radio on his side table. His body was hard and aching, his mind awhirl with lustful thoughts, his heart awash in emotion. He knew he wouldn't sleep much because his body was too awake, his mind too alert for sleep. And he wanted to think about the woman who was consuming his every waking moment. He wanted her with a fierceness that took his breath away. It was unsettling for a man who had prided himself on his absolute control of his emotions and his behavior to find that he was completely out of control whenever Karen appeared, in person or in thought.

He wondered if she was asleep and what her nightie looked like under that demure dressing gown. He wondered if she slept on her back or belly or side, if she talked in her sleep, if she thrashed about, if she would hog the covers. He wondered what her naked body would look like in the moonlight that was now beginning to illuminate the darkness of his room.

His cock swelled painfully in the loose shorts he wore, and he rubbed it absently, for once too caught up in thoughts of the kisses he had shared with her to be much interested in relieving the ache they caused. He could still feel the plumpness, taste the juicy sweetness, and he thirsted for more. He had decided he would take her for a drive around the neighboring country tomorrow, then stop for a pub lunch before coming back in time for dinner with Jannie and Duncan. He hoped she would let him forget himself again and kiss her senseless.

It was almost dawn before he dropped off and later was wakened by the sound of the shower in the adjoining bathroom. Karen was singing, and her voice wafted to him over the sound of the water, making him hard as a board again. He sat up groaning and tried to hear the song she was singing, but he couldn't make out the tune. *Perhaps it's a good thing,* he thought as he looked out his window to the garden below. Jannie was out and about filling the bird feeder and plucking dry leaves from the rose bushes. The dogs followed her—she had kept them confined for the party, and they were obviously enjoying their renewed freedom—snapping gleefully at dragonflies and roughhousing with each other.

The shower stopped, and he did his best to keep his thoughts on the animals outside, on the bright morning, on anything but the thought of

Karen's wet, naked body. When he felt enough time had elapsed, he knocked on the door, and receiving no reply, went in to have his own shower, and to endeavor to calm his body. He could not appear for breakfast with an erection, which would be noticeable even in the jeans he had decided to wear for a change. By the time he was ready to face the world, and especially his cousin and Karen, his wet hair brushed back and his jaw smooth, his body was as calm as it would get. He put his cell phone, wallet, and keys in the pockets of his jeans and went downstairs.

Karen was at the stove, and the smell of bacon made his mouth water. Jannie was nowhere in sight, and he knew that Duncan had already gone for the day, having a conference to attend two hours away.

"Good morning!" he said cheerfully, waiting for her to turn around so he could drown himself in her liquid brown eyes.

She was wearing a lovely sundress that clung to her curves. She turned as he spoke, and a pretty blush stole up her cheeks. He knew she was remembering the kisses they had shared at bedtime, and he wondered if she, like he, was wishing they could share good morning ones as well. She smiled at him and turned back to the stove, no doubt hiding from him. The thought made his own smile widen.

"I'm making breakfast," she explained, "so Jannie can spend some time in the garden before the sun gets too hot. She told me she has an appointment this afternoon, so the gardening can't wait." She turned again to look over her shoulder at him for a brief moment, and added, "I hope you like bacon, eggs, and pancakes."

"Yes, I do," he replied. "How can I help you?"

"I don't know how to make coffee if it's not instant. Can you handle that? Jannie says she has coffee in the morning and tea in the afternoon and evening. Apparently, Duncan took the first pot she made with him!"

Karen kept her back to him, and he resisted the urge to chuckle aloud. The last thing he expected was for her to be suddenly shy with him, but he supposed he understood. They had been only friends online until their first kiss. Now they seemed to be morphing into something much more, and he understood her reluctance to let things get out of control. They were adults, not hormonal teenagers, though his reactions tried to prove otherwise. His body was tight, the jeans feeling constricting as he fought for control. Just the thought that she was in a similar situation turned him on more than he could remember being, apart from their shared kisses last evening.

"I can do that for you," he said, glad of something to do to occupy his mind, and set about making coffee, being sure to stay out of her way as she went to the refrigerator and the bread bin. He helped her lay the table for three and poured the fresh-brewed coffee into the tall pot, placing it on the table as she went to get Jannie. He fetched cream and sugar for the table as well, then waited for the women to return.

The dogs came bounding back inside ahead of the two women and danced around him happily. He bent to scratch behind their ears and let himself be licked.

"They're happy to see you again, Peter!" Jannie exclaimed with a laugh. "We so rarely have visitors these days, and they do love to be sociable!"

"Scrooge would love to play with them, I'm sure!" he replied, laughing as Constable, the older of the two Dalmatians, danced around Karen's legs. He was a bit lame with age, but his rear end didn't seem to care as he shared his affection with the new person. Peter saw the look that came and went in Karen's eyes as he washed his hands, and he realized suddenly that she had not moved once the dog began to play with her.

"Not a dog lover?" he asked softly, so only she heard him.

"I'm sorry. Does it show?" She stood perfectly still as though she knew she would not be hurt if she played the role of a statue.

"It's okay. Constable won't hurt you," he tried to reassure her. "Come and sit."

He went to escort her to the table and waited until she was seated before sitting himself across from her. The dogs had been called for their own food, and so were out of the way. Jannie joined them, and they dug into the repast. The food was good, and Peter realized he was starving.

"Thanks for making breakfast, Karen," Jannie said, breaking the companionable silence between them. "I haven't been much of a hostess this morning, but I'm glad you're a good sort!" She chuckled and looked expectantly at her cousin. "So, what are the plans for the rest of the weekend, Peter?"

"I'm taking Karen for a bit of a drive," he answered, wiping his lips on a napkin. "We'll have lunch in a pub somewhere and be home in time for dinner." He looked at Karen as he spoke. "Is that alright with you?"

She smiled at them both. "Of course! I've never been here before, so a drive sounds perfect."

"Tomorrow, I'll take her back home on my way back to Leeuwarden." He swallowed the last of his coffee and poured himself a second cup.

"Will you be leaving early?" Jannie wanted to know. "I'll need to pack you both lunch for the journey and make breakfast, too."

"Oh, maybe around ten in the morning," he replied. He could almost see the wheels turning in his cousin's busy brain as she tried to find ways to prolong the time he spent with Karen. He knew she liked the woman he had already begun to develop deep feelings for, and in her capacity as older sister, she would do everything in her power to see him happy. He smiled at her, as if to let her know he knew what she was up to, and asked Karen, "Will you be ready to go in half an hour?"

"Yes, of course!" She finished the food on her plate and refused Jannie's offer of seconds, smiling into her coffee as though she also had an inkling of Jannie's intentions.

"Will you take her to see Blenheim Palace, Peter? It's beautiful at any time of year!" Jannie enthused. "The Summer Outdoor Theatre has just begun its performances, too, in case you want to eschew dinner at home for some Shakespeare or whatever they have in store."

"I had forgotten about that!" Peter considered it as he drained his cup again. "Can you pack us one of your splendid picnic suppers, Jannie? We'll come back in time for a rest before the play."

Jannie's eyes twinkled with delight. "Lovely! I'll do you proud, love." She stood and began clearing the table. "Now go on and have a lovely day roaming about!"

CHAPTER 12

B efore too much longer, Peter was settling Karen into the passenger seat of his car and heading out. He stopped for gas, then began a leisurely tour of the neighborhood, showing off the town he had come to love and the neighboring little village where Winston Churchill was buried in the churchyard. He took her to visit Blenheim Palace, so she would have some sense of what the quality lived like, at least some of the time. They spent some time in the gardens because Karen declared herself in need of fresh air.

"I'm sure if I return here, I'll take more of an interest in the interior," she said as they walked through the beautiful grounds.

She took lots of pictures on her cell phone, and he took some of her, unbeknownst to her, loving the way she looked in the wide-skirted dress among the flowers and on the pathways of the gardens. She wanted a turn in the maze, and he was delighted that she held his hand as they traversed the puzzling space, as though she didn't want to lose her way and trusted him to bring her back to safety. He took a picture of their hands entwined while she was distracted by thoughts of which way to go next. Holding his hand was an endearing gesture of which he was sure she was entirely unaware, and he did nothing to cause her to remark upon it. He loved the way her soft hand felt in his, and he had to remind himself more than once not to caress her with his thumb or bring it to his lips for a kiss. The day was pleasantly warm, and by the time she had had enough of the great outdoors, they were both more than ready for a drink and some lunch.

Having found a table in the courtyard garden of a favorite local pub, Peter watched as Karen sipped her drink and perused the menu. Her cheeks were warm from the time spent in the sun, and there was a faint sheen of perspiration on her upper lip that teased his senses. He wanted to taste it, to taste her again, but he also wanted to enjoy this quiet time with her without the strain of out-of-control emotions. They shared a pitcher of lemonade and ate hearty sandwiches made with thick slices of bread slathered with creamy butter and fat pieces of sharp Cheddar cheese.

"It's such a beautiful day!" she enthused as she sat back, relaxed, watching the other diners.

"It is, isn't it?" he replied. "I hope the evening is as fair for our plans."

"I'm not sure I have anything to wear," she said. "Perhaps I should buy myself something in the shops before we go back."

"I'm sure what you're wearing now is fine, Karen," he said, allowing himself to look at her from her eyes to her chest. "You look beautiful!"

He watched her cover her lips with the napkin, ostensibly to wipe them, but more, he sensed, to hide them from his hungry scrutiny.

"If you'd like to do a bit of shopping before we go home, I'll be happy to take you," he added and looked away, letting her off the hook for now. He fully intended to kiss her again before the day was over, so he could afford to be generous now and allow her to relax again.

After lunch, she declared herself so full that she needed a walk to work it off, so they strolled down Market Street, visiting the shops, and she bought herself a bracelet she admired in a little boutique. She also bought a gift for Jannie—a pashmina shawl—and worried that she didn't know what to buy for Duncan.

"Don't worry about that," he reassured her. "Neither of them is expecting anything from you."

He smiled at her and let her wander off on her own so he could pick up the scarf he had seen that would go beautifully with the dress she was wearing as well as the perfect chain for the pendant he had bought her two months earlier. She was paying for her purchases as he approached the cash register, and he smiled at her as she waited for him to pay for his own. They drove back in companionable silence, and as soon as he got to his room, he transferred the pendant from the leather strap to the chain he had just bought, and put it aside for later. Before long, he was knocking on her door again, waiting anxiously for her to admit him.

"May I come in?" he asked when she finally opened the door. He tried not to react to the sight of her in her dressing gown from the night before. "I have something for you."

Karen stepped back, allowing him to enter, and he walked into the center of the room.

"You were worried about what to wear later, so I thought this might add a little something to your dress and also be another layer to keep you warm, in case it gets chilly."

He handed her the tissue-wrapped scarf and watched as she unwrapped it and stared. The scarf was silk, a pretty mixture of golds and reds and blues, slashes of color that would enhance any number of things that she might wear, but that would pick up the gold highlights in the dress she had taken off. He knew he should feel guilty for disturbing her when she clearly had undressed so she could rest, but he could feel nothing but a rising desire to see what was under the thin dressing gown, and a wish that it were thin enough to let him see through it.

"Oh my! How thoughtful of you, Peter! It's beautiful! Thank you. You're very kind."

He listened to her gush, and knew she was nervous, probably because she recognized the look he was giving her for what it was—the intention to kiss her mindless. He didn't wait for her to protest his desires but stepped closer and kissed her without touching her anywhere else but on those luscious lips. He knew that if he held her, he would forget where he was, that her door was open for anyone who happened by to see, and that he would ravish her. He searched her mouth as though she had treasure hidden in it, and his body tightened when she groaned. He answered her groan with his own, needing so much more than one kiss and sternly denying himself.

"I'm glad you like it, *liefje*," he whispered against her lips. "I'll let you get some rest now. See you later," he said, smiling into her eyes.

She licked her lips and touched his dimple again, and the caress broke the thread of his control.

"Karen, I want you more with every minute I spend with you. Don't tempt me, love!" he begged her but wrapped his arms around her anyway and kissed her some more.

He was hungry for her, and by the way she wrapped her arms around his neck and pulled his head down to her, she was for him, too. He drank from her and pulled her body hard into his own, letting her feel him, letting himself feel her, fighting to keep from writhing against her in an agony of need and lust.

"Get some rest, baby." He rested his lips on hers fleetingly one more time and walked out before he lost it completely.

Karen watched him go but could not seem to move for a minute after he disappeared. She stood trembling in the middle of the room, wanting him with a fierceness that shook her, though it no longer surprised her. She had loved to feel his hard body, all muscles and desire, pressed against her earlier, and she knew he was stopping himself from rubbing against her as she had been doing herself. It wouldn't do to get physical in his cousin's house. When they made love, she wanted it to be where no one could have any reason to care what two people who were falling in love were doing behind closed doors.

Falling in love ... she knew she was. *How could it be possible,* she wondered as she closed the door and lay on the bed, *that two people who barely know each other could be falling in love so soon?* It was beyond her understanding, and she remembered as she set her cell phone alarm to six and drifted off to sleep that her aunt had once told her that no one can choose who to love or when. Karen supposed she was right. Unbidden, Niall McLaren came to mind. He was as handsome as Peter, bolder, brassier, the sort of man for whom most women fell head over heels. And yet, he had sparked nothing more in her than warm feelings of friendship. It was Peter who made her think raunchy thoughts, Peter who made her hot all over, Peter who starred in her wet dreams.

The chiming clock on her phone dragged her out of sleep, and she took a second to recall where she was. It was time to get ready for her evening. She had hung the dress up to air, and now with the scarf Peter had given her, she would look presentable for an evening out. She made sure no one was in the bathroom before going in to wash her face and brush her teeth. Back in her room, she applied makeup again, put the dress back on, and swathed the scarf just so around her neck and shoulders. Spritzing herself with her favorite fragrance, and taking Jannie's gift with her, she went back downstairs to wait for him.

Jannie was standing at the kitchen table putting the last few items into the picnic basket. She looked up as Karen entered.

"What a lovely picture you make, my dear!" she said. "I'll have to take a photo of you and Peter when he comes down!"

Karen smiled at her, finding her obvious matchmaking amusing. "Peter bought me this scarf to wear this evening as I was moaning about not having something different to wear out," she explained to Jannie. "That's why the dress shines now!"

"He certainly has good taste, doesn't he, my dear?" Jannie replied with a smile. Turning away for a moment, she took up a small pack and turned back to place it in the basket. "There now. That's ready!" She looked up at Karen and added, "I'm sure you'll have a lovely time this evening. The performances are usually stellar, you know."

"I bought you something as well," Karen said and handed her the gift. "I hope you like it."

Jannie unwrapped the shawl and declared herself perfectly pleased with it. "You needn't have bought me a thing," she added with a wide smile, "but I appreciate your thoughtfulness, my dear!"

Peter walked in at that moment, and Karen turned to smile a welcome at him.

"I think Jannie has packed food to feed the five thousand, Peter," she joked as he approached.

He laughed as he surveyed the contents of the basket, and Jannie chuckled.

"You had a long walk today, I'm sure, and food keeps your bones warm on chilly evenings!" She was unrepentant, which made Karen laugh aloud.

"Is there wine, Jannie?" Peter asked.

"Of course, love! And some cheese for afters."

Karen looked at her. "Afters?" she wondered.

"After dinner, my dear. I didn't have much by way of dessert, but cheese is always a good thing to pair with grapes. I hope you'll like that?" She

There was concern in her voice, which Karen hastened to address. "It sounds perfect, Jannie. Thank you!"

Peter picked up the basket and turned to Karen. "Shall we go?" he invited her, but before she could follow him, Jannie interrupted.

"Come on, then, let's have a shot of you!"

She had concealed her camera on the kitchen counter, and now she retrieved it and bid them smile at her. Satisfied with their facial expressions, she snapped the shot, looked at it, and declared herself happy with the results. She showed it to them and promised to send a copy to Peter before she went to bed. Finally, Karen followed Peter out to the car, carrying the two lawn chairs Jannie had placed by the front door.

Parking and finding their way to a suitable spot for picnicking and seeing the stage took more time than Karen had anticipated, and they had just settled into their lawn chairs when the performance began. The play was Shakespeare's *Much Ado About Nothing*, which they both thoroughly enjoyed from start to finish. The actors were well cast, and the play innovatively interpreted. As it progressed, they feasted on steak and kidney pie with greens, a full-bodied port, and cleansed their palates with cheese and grapes.

Karen took the opportunity to watch the others around her, noting the families, the couples, and even a lone watcher or two in amongst the crowd. Everyone seemed to be enjoying the performance equally well. When Beatrice and Benedick kissed each other around their teasing words at the end, Karen felt Peter's eyes on her and turned to see the hungry look on his face again. She smiled and turned her attention back to the stage. By the time the cast was taking its bows, she had completely relaxed. She helped Peter to pack up the basket, though he insisted on leaving the wine and glasses on top.

"For a final toast before we go back home," he had said by way of explanation.

Now, they were walking back to the car, and Peter was greeted by a few people who recognized him. She could feel their eyes on her and could almost hear them wondering who she was. She was glad he didn't stop to talk as she could not have borne their scrutiny. Once the things had been packed securely in the trunk, Peter handed her the unfinished bottle of wine and the two glasses and settled her in the passenger seat.

"There's a little clearing behind Jannie's house," he said, starting the engine, "where we can sit and watch the night. I'm not quite ready to go back home yet, are you?" He turned to her, his hands on the wheel, and waited.

"Not if you're not," she answered him, hoping she didn't sound coy or simpering. She wanted to be careful, but she could feel the tension that the evening's outing had kept at bay building again between them, and she didn't want to douse it unless he did.

He nodded and drove off, arriving at the small clearing and shutting off the engine. Karen could see Jannie's house behind her, a lone light on, in the kitchen she imagined. She listened to the sound of wine being poured and turned to accept her glass from Peter.

"I'd like to propose a toast," he began, "to a most beautiful woman."

Karen chuckled. "I don't think you can expect me to raise a glass to that, Peter!" she retorted. "Perhaps something else, more specific?"

He smiled at her. "What do you suggest, then?"

"Well," she hesitated, considering, "why are you toasting this woman?" She wanted to test him, to see what he would say.

"She's intelligent, feisty, funny," he began, and when she smirked at him, he continued, "and I'm falling in love with her."

Trying not to show her shock at his admission, and endeavoring to keep from spilling the contents of her glass, she said, "A toast to newfound love, then?"

Her voice was low and husky, but she couldn't help that. She was floored by his confession and unprepared to respond as she knew she should. She needed a few moments to gather herself, to calm her quaking nerves, to …

"To newfound love!" he said, interrupting her thoughts. He watched her, not doing anything, just waiting.

"To newfound love!" she echoed in a shaky voice and lowered her eyes from his to take a gulp of wine. Liquid courage, she knew, but she needed it right then.

She felt his hand on hers as he took her glass, and she noticed for the first time that he did not have one. She watched him turn it so his lips would rest where hers had been, then he took a sip. Her breath hitched in her throat, and she stared helplessly into his face, watching his head descend, opening her mouth to receive his kiss. She suckled his tongue as he did hers and rested her hands on his broad, hard chest, feeling his heart racing under her fingertips.

"I have something else for you," he murmured, his hand trembling on her cheek as he drew away from her at last.

He finished the wine in the glass that he had managed to hold steady and put it on the dashboard. Then, switching on the ceiling light, he reached into the glove compartment in front of her and withdrew a jeweler's box. Karen's heart beat rapidly. It was too big to be a ring box, but she couldn't tell what it could be from the size. It didn't look long enough to be a necklace, but then again, what did she know? She was not in the habit of receiving gifts from men, particularly gifts of jewelry.

"I bought this for you when we were in London," he began, "on the day after we had supper together. I hope you like it."

He held out the box to her, and Karen took it, opening it immediately to reveal a brilliant crystal pendant attached to a shimmering silver chain. She picked up the chain, a sturdy, beautiful herringbone necklace and felt the weight of the crystal. It was a faceted oval and sparkled beautifully in the dim light.

"Oh Peter, it's lovely!" She looked up at him, and on an impulse, raised her lips to thank him with a kiss. "Thank you!" she whispered when she drew her mouth from his.

"You're welcome," he whispered back and put a finger under her chin. "If I asked, would you give me a longer thank you?" he teased.

He chuckled when she smiled at him and kissed him again, and she felt herself grow damp at the way his kiss went from friendly to hungry. She let the gift fall back into the box so she could cup his cheeks and kiss him back the way she wanted to and show him that she felt the same way that he did. They held each other tenderly but kissed wildly, and before long, Karen was pulling away to drag in a ragged breath.

Placing her fingers over his warm lips, even as he sought to capture hers again, she said, "I'd like you to put it on me, please, love."

She let the endearment slip, a kind of advance notice of her feelings, and looked him in the eye. He pushed through her fingers and ate at her lips again, and Karen gave herself up to the fire that threatened to consume them both.

"*Liefje!*" His breath was warm on her mouth, his pulse racing when she laid her head on his shoulder. "Tell me, do you feel the same way I do?"

Karen smiled. "I'm sure you know I do, Peter!"

"Tell me, *liefje!*" he prompted. "Say the words!" He caressed her lips with his thumb to encourage her.

"I'm falling in love with you, too!"

He sucked the words off her lips then, pulling her closer to him, taking the kisses she willingly gave him.

"I think perhaps we should go in now," Peter said at last, pulling away from her. "Here, let me put that on for you first." He took the necklace from the box in her lap and pulled her head down so he could put it on. Lifting her chin, he touched his hand to the pendant. "Okay?" he asked.

When she nodded, he stole one last kiss before starting the car and driving them the two minutes home. Duncan was already in, and Karen braced herself for meeting her hosts before she could go to bed. The voices in the kitchen stopped for a split second when they walked in, then the conversation resumed. Peter steered her up by the front stairs, stopping before her door to wish her a good night.

"I'll see you in the morning, baby. Sleep well. Good night."

He kissed her cheek and walked away, bypassing his room and going down to the kitchen by the back stairs. She assumed he would make her excuses for her, and she was grateful. She wasn't ready yet to face his matchmaking cousin. Instead, she stripped and hurried through her shower before crawling into bed, her body still tingling from the promise in his kisses. The shower had not cooled her ardor, and as she drifted off to sleep, she wondered what he had told them.

CHAPTER 13

K aren did not wake until the sun was high in the sky, having slept through her phone's alarm. Her eyes snapped open only when there was a discreet knock at her door, and Jannie's voice called her for breakfast.

"I'll be a bit late, Jannie," she stuttered. "Please go on without me!"

She listened to Jannie's demur with half an ear, choosing instead to pack her bag, rush through her morning routine, and dress hurriedly. She was only a half an hour late as she pulled her luggage down the back stairs with her to the kitchen. The others were sitting around the table when she walked in, but Jannie rose immediately and retrieved a plate from the warming oven.

"Have a seat, dear!" she invited Karen, who sat gratefully in the only other chair available. "I see Peter wore you out yesterday, eh?" Jannie smiled and added, "I hope you slept well!"

Karen fought the blush that rose in her cheeks at the thought of Peter wearing her out and replied,

"Like a log, apparently. I slept right through my alarm! I'm sorry to be late!"

"No worries," Peter assured her. "We're right on time. Take your time and enjoy your breakfast. I'll just do my own packing now. See you in a bit!"

He left her to the tender mercies of his cousins who began to speak almost at once.

"I hope you enjoyed your time here," Jannie said.

"You must come again, and bring Peter with you!" Duncan teased.

Karen laughed. "Shouldn't that be the other way around?"

"We understand you didn't take in the sights inside Blenheim Palace, so we will take it as read that you'll be back for that!" Duncan explained. "We're happy to have met you, Karen," he added, "and we wish you the best."

His last comment was made with an intonation that told Karen he and his wife were very worried about their cousin and hoped she would be the answer they wanted for him. She didn't know how to answer the underlying message, so she just said thank you and left it at that. Peter returned as she was finishing her orange juice, and she stood up to put her dishes in the sink.

"No, that's quite all right, my dear. I'll take care of these!" Jannie took the things out of her hands and put them in the sink, then crossed to Peter, wrapping her arms around him and giving him a sound kiss on each cheek. "It was lovely to have you," she told him. "I'll call you about the reunion in Scotland as soon as I have more information."

"It was lovely to be here, Jannie," he answered and walked over to shake Duncan's hand. "I look forward to hearing about the family reunion."

He picked up her suitcase, and they all walked out to the car, where final goodbyes were said, and Karen found herself embraced by both Jannie and Duncan.

"Have a safe journey!" Duncan called as they drove off. Karen waved at the couple, then turned back in her seat. She watched the houses and shops go by and enjoyed the look of the countryside for a while, thinking about his cousin and her husband.

"They're not very English, are they?" she commented after a while, with a smile.

"Well, no, they're not. Not at all! Jannie is Dutch, of course, and Duncan ... well, let's just say that he's not your average Englishman!" Peter replied with a chuckle. "Why did you say that?"

"They're very demonstrative. I've never known English people—the few I do know—to be so touchy-feely and friendly. I was quite surprised when they both hugged me goodbye just now!" She laughed softly. "Whatever happened to that stiff upper lip?"

Peter laughed aloud at that and said, "Well, Jannie was always demonstrative, even as a child, and I think her being a nurturer sort of requires that, don't you? As to Duncan, I guess Jannie's warmth has rubbed off on him." He paused for a moment to negotiate their turn onto the highway from the roundabout, then added, "I have to say, though, that I think their response to you is largely because of me."

"You have lovely relatives, Peter, and it's so nice to see how much they love you!"

"It's nice to be loved," he murmured almost nonchalantly, but she felt his eyes on her briefly when he said it, and she immediately recalled their declarations of love the night before. Her hand stole up to touch the heavy glass pendant nestled in her warm cleavage as she wondered why he had bought her the gift so soon in their acquaintance.

"I think I started falling for you the moment you stumbled into my arms, and after our second meeting, I wanted something tangible to record my feelings," he said, making her wonder if she had spoken her question aloud.

He reached over and took her hand in his, lacing his fingers through hers and resting their joined hands on his thigh. His own was big and warm, engulfing hers in a possessive and comforting grip, making her feel needed and cherished more than any words he might have said just then. She resisted the urge to raise his hand to her lips and felt herself grow hot when he did just that, planting a sensual kiss in the middle of her palm.

"What will you be doing till the end of June when I'm free again?" he asked after a long silence.

"House hunting," she said immediately. "I love my brother, and his lady is very sweet, but I don't want to cramp their style any longer than I need to. Besides, I need to turn my own key again. This living with a concern for my hours and other idiosyncrasies is very wearing on the nerves."

Peter chuckled at her evident annoyance. "Where are you planning to live? Close to your brother?"

"No, I'm not one for big cities. I prefer small towns or even the country. But I don't know anything about good places for someone like me to live in this country, so I'm relying on George and Toni to help me find something suitable within my means."

She tried to keep the worry out of her voice. The online editing business she had begun before she moved to Birmingham was just beginning to take off, so she could live anywhere, technically. But the idea of being in a completely strange place alone was unusually uncomfortable to her, and she was irritated by the unsettled feelings that swamped her whenever she thought about it.

"If you like, I can ask Jannie for suggestions," Peter offered soothingly as though he could sense her unease.

She chuckled. "I'm sure they'll be only too eager to suggest I move to Woodstock!" she said.

"I suppose you may be right," he answered on a laugh. "Would that be so bad?"

His voice was carefully neutral, but Karen sensed he might not be as disinterested as he wanted to appear. She didn't want to appear to be snubbing his relatives, especially since she liked them well enough, but the last thing she wanted at this point in her life was more well-meaning but nosy relatives minding her business with her. She assumed a nonchalant air.

"Living in Woodstock, you mean? Probably not. But I want to see what else is available that might appeal to me more. You never can tell, you know, and I don't want to settle for the first good thing that comes along when there might be better out there."

He let her answer rest, for which she was grateful. Their feelings for each other were still too new to withstand an argument, especially one over something trivial. Instead, he turned the conversation over to a discussion of summer plans. She listened with half an ear, feeling unaccountably drowsy and having to force herself to stay alert. It was a hard battle, one she clearly lost when she heard him speaking through a kind of fogbank in her head.

"If you're tired, why don't you push the seat back and have a nap, Karen? We have another hour yet to Birmingham."

She blushed deeply and began to stammer out a denial when he raised her hand to his lips again, kissing her palm warmly.

"It's all right, *liefje*. I'll wake you when we get there."

She wanted to insist that she was okay, but it seemed foolish, given that she must have dozed off enough for him to notice at least once before now, so she reluctantly adjusted the seat and rested her head back, though she tried valiantly to keep her eyes open. It was with some surprise, then, that she felt herself being gently shaken awake an hour later. The car had stopped, and Peter was looking at her, amusement and affection in his eyes. She closed her mouth, which she found, to her horror, had been gaping open. *Did I snore? Drool?* The thought of being so vulnerable and open to him was mortifying.

Hard on the heels of that thought was that she had apparently crossed a barrier as she had gone and slept with him without the benefit of a bed. And in the front seat of a car, no less! A giggle escaped unwittingly, and she cleared her throat when Peter's eyes sharpened on her.

"Was the dream amusing, then?" he asked.

"Dream?" she answered. "Was I dreaming?" She had no recollection of doing any such thing.

"Either that or you are a sleep talker," he replied, smiling at her.

"If I was dreaming, I don't remember it now," she said and straightened the seat.

She refused to ask him what she had said, and he didn't seem inclined to tell her, which suited her just fine. He got out of the car and came round to help her out, then went to retrieve her suitcase from the trunk. They walked together up the short path to the front door, which she quickly opened. No one was home, she knew. George and Elaine always went out on Sunday afternoons and didn't come back until very late, so she'd be on her own for a while. From nowhere, the thought came to her that it would have been nice if Peter didn't have to go back so soon. They could be alone together for a few hours. She hurried ahead of him to hide her warming cheeks from his gaze and asked him to put the case by the closet door.

"Thank you for inviting me out, Peter," she said, turning to face him when her cheeks cooled. "I had a lovely time!"

He put the case down and walked with her to the door, which he had closed behind him when they entered.

"So did I, Karen," he murmured and took her hands in his. "I'd like to do it again soon if you don't mind."

He looked deeply into her eyes and lowered his head, kissing her slowly, deeply, taking his time, not apparently worried that he might be interrupted. He pulled her fully into his arms, letting her mouth go only long enough to let them each catch a breath before retaking it, sucking her lips in, swirling his tongue around them before plunging in to drink from her again. Karen's knees buckled when he pulled her hips into his own, and she felt his hardness pressed against her. She had had no inkling that he had been aroused, and she wondered vaguely when that had happened.

"There's a music festival happening in my neck of the woods in July. Would you like to come and share it with me? You could spend the weekend at my place, so there would be no cost to you."

He didn't wait for her answer but seemed impatient to get back to his feast, and Karen let him have his fill of her lips and tongue. The grandfather clock ticked sedately, but they were oblivious to the passage of time. Their kisses grew more fevered, their hands more frenzied, their breathing more labored. They swayed against each other, and Karen moaned in disappointment when Peter drew away from her.

"If I stay any longer, we both know where this will end," he said, kissing a trail down the side of her neck to her throat, smiling when she giggled. "And I find myself unwilling to make love to you for the first time in your brother's house." He nipped her neck playfully and chuckled when she giggled again.

"Have I found a sweet spot, then?" he wondered, lowering his head to breathe on her there and nipping her earlobe.

"I'm ticklish," she admitted and exhaled when he stroked her back as he kissed her down to her inviting breasts, hidden beneath the T-shirt she wore. He raised his head to gaze at them, squeezing the plump flesh between suddenly trembling hands.

"I'll send you the details of the festival as soon as I get home," he told her, his eyes raised to hers, the hunger in them almost hypnotizing her. "I want you to come, love," he added, and Karen knew he wasn't just talking about her visit. She blushed, and he pushed his hips against hers one more time before putting her away from him.

"I'll call you when I get home, love, okay?" He kissed her lips again, and she watched him get back into the car and drive away.

Hours later, when Peter finally opened the door to his apartment, he was weary but determined to call Karen before he went to bed. He dropped his case on the bed and pulled his cell phone out of his pocket. Before long, he heard her now familiar voice.

"Hello!"

"Karen, I'm home!" he said without preamble. "Feeling a bit whipped, and I have work tomorrow, so I won't stay long tonight."

"That's okay, Peter. I understand!" she answered him, and he could just picture the smile on her face as she reassured him.

"I'll send the details of the music festival tomorrow before I go to work, and then we can discuss it further if that's okay with you."

"Certainly," she said. "Now go to bed! I work from home, so my commute is nonexistent!"

"Goodnight, baby!" he murmured. "Sweet dreams!"

"And the same to you, love!" she replied.

He hung up and went to get Scrooge from the neighbor who had kindly watched him, glad that he had had his evening constitutional, so Peter wouldn't have to leave the apartment again. He bore the dog's excited welcome home, fed and watered him, and after a quick shower, he toppled into bed. He didn't know when he fell asleep, but the dream that woke him had him hard and aching, his cock in hand, dripping precum on himself and his sheets. He tried to slow his breathing, but he felt as though he were still in the dream, reaching a roaring climax in Karen's arms. The cool night air chilled his heated skin as he rose to clean himself.

The chiming clock proclaimed the hour to be two, but he was so wired he was afraid he wouldn't be able to go back to sleep. Taking his laptop back to bed, he sat with his back against the headboard and checked his emails. There was a message from Karen, which he opened eagerly.

"Hi Peter," it said. *"I'm glad you've arrived home safely. I just wanted to thank you again for inviting me to meet your family. I had a really lovely time. I'm looking forward to seeing you again on your home turf. Rest well, and sweet dreams. Karen."*

Taking a deep breath, he searched online for the information he needed and answered her email.

Dear Karen,

I woke up unexpectedly—I had been dreaming of you!—and found your message. I'm glad you had fun. So did I, and I too can't wait for the next time we can be together. The event takes place on July 10 and 11. I'll be on holiday by then and wouldn't mind spending more than a weekend with you. Are you up for that? Let me know, and I can arrange to show you

*more. Sleep well, yourself, and sweet
dreams, liefje!*

Peter.

He clicked send and closed the laptop, setting
it aside before lying down again and praying for
sleep. He woke late and had to rush through his
morning routines, missing his cup of coffee and
barely making it to work on time. He taught all
his classes, attended meetings scheduled for the
afternoon, and by the end of the day, he was ready
for home. Scrooge was waiting to be walked—he
had curtailed the dog's morning run—and he felt
it best to get it over with so he could get some
marking done, prepare for the tests he would
be giving, and hopefully have time left over to
call Karen.

By the time he was done, it was late, and he
wondered if he should try her. But he needed to
hear her voice again, and he promised himself to
keep it short. He dialed her number and waited a
heartbeat before she answered.

"Hello, Peter!" she answered.

"How did you know it was me?" he
asked, smiling.

"Caller ID ... your name is attached to your
number," she explained. "How are you? Is everything all right?"

She sounded anxious, and he hastened to
reassure her. "Yes, I'm alright, and everything is

fine. I just needed to hear you again." He stopped abruptly and waited to hear what she would say.

"I miss you too, Peter!"

He could hear the smile in her voice. "Did you read my email?" he wanted to know.

"Yes, and I can be there for as long as you want," she said.

"Mmmmm ... that sounds quite inviting, baby." He dropped his voice, although he was alone, aware that he might sound seductive and not caring. "I can make all the arrangements for you, if you like," he offered.

"What do you mean?" she asked, clearly puzzled.

"I'll book the flight if you want me to."

"I wouldn't dream of asking you to pay my fare, Peter!" she exclaimed, scandalized. "I can afford it!"

"You're not asking me. I'm offering. I know you can afford it, *liefje*, but I want to. Please? It would make me happy."

He waited again, almost hearing the wheels turning in her head and praying that she would give in to him on this. He knew she had no steady income at the moment, and as he was the one wanting her to come to him, it seemed only right to foot the bill.

"Can we compromise?" she asked. "You can book it and pay for it, but I'll return half the cost to you when I get there. How's that?"

"You mean, go Dutch?" he asked on a laugh.

He would take whatever she was willing to give, knowing that he would be able to spend whatever he liked on her when she got there, without her even knowing about it. He heard her answering laugh.

"Good one!" she congratulated him. "You're quick, aren't you?"

"When I have to be," he conceded. He paused, needing to do more than talk shop. He wanted to be tender, romantic, sensual before he said good-night. "I'll be thinking of you when I go to sleep in a bit," he said. "My dreams last night were wonderful!"

"Oh ... tell me, please?" He liked the way she sounded.

"Think back to yesterday or the night before. Feel me pressed against you. Can you do that?" He spoke hoarsely and had to clear his throat to continue. "In my dream, we made love."

He listened to her silence with a knowing smile. He hadn't meant to start this, but he wished she were with him, so he could end it the way he had dreamt.

"Was I any good?" she asked, surprising him into a husky chuckle.

"You rocked my world, *liefje*!"

She inhaled deeply, and Peter could almost feel her gathering herself before she spoke. "I don't remember most of my dreams," she said, "and the ones that I do remember are nightmares. So, I'll settle for hearing about your dreams!"

He smiled. "If I have any others, I'll be sure to share them with you."

The clock chimed the hour. He sighed. He needed to get some more rest. "I have to go now, baby. I'm sorry! I'll call you earlier tomorrow, I promise."

"Okay. Sleep well, love!"

"I will, now, baby. Sweet dreams yourself. Goodnight!"

CHAPTER 14

The next three weeks flew by with calls to Karen at night and testing and final end-of-year activities at school. He looked forward to their evening talks, each day growing bolder, each conversation hotter until he thought he would burst with desire for her. Finally, it was the night before she was to arrive, and he called to tell her goodnight, as usual.

"Are you ready for me?" he asked her.

"I don't know," she answered him, chuckling softly, "but I'm ready to come and find out!"

"I'll be waiting, sweetie, with open arms."

"I loved it when you held me before," she confessed.

"Not as much as I loved holding you and kissing you," he countered. "And I can't wait to do it again! Get some sleep, love. I'll see you tomorrow morning."

The hours to her arrival seemed to Peter to crawl, but eventually, he saw her pulling her suitcase—he still marveled that she travelled so lightly!—and he hurried to meet her. When he stood before her, her scent assailed him, and he pulled her into his arms and kissed her, uncaring of the passersby. Need swamped him, and he barely remembered where he was.

"Hello there," he said shakily when he raised his head. "Welcome back!"

Karen smiled at him and relinquished her suitcase, letting him hold her hand and lead her out to his car. He didn't let her go for the ride back to his home, and she barely noticed the scenery they drove through. She was so taken with the way his hand felt engulfing hers, the way his lips made her tingle and grow warm where he had pressed his mouth, the way his hard thigh felt beneath her fingers, the way his scent curled around her and stole inside her. She was so turned on by being near him that she could barely process a thought. The instant she had seen him approach her at the airport, she felt as though all the air had been sucked out of the building, and only his kiss of welcome had brought it all back in a rush.

He was speaking, and she shook herself to get her focus back. "I'm sorry … I was …" she hesitated, not wanting to tell him that she hadn't been paying attention.

"I know," he said, and she had the feeling he did. "How was the flight?" he asked.

"Okay, which I am grateful for, as I hate flying!"

He told her about the towns they drove through, introduced her to the dykes they drove over, and finally stopped before the building where he lived.

They had passed by fancy hotels, specialty shops, and driven beside canals to get there. Karen loved the old world feel of the city, and the old buildings looked perfectly charming and begged to be visited. She could see herself exploring the city on foot with Peter as her guide. She turned her attention to the building they had stopped in front of on a narrow street full of shops and cafes. The logo told her it was a bookstore, though the words meant nothing to her.

"You live in a bookshop?" she asked incredulously.

"I live above it, in the apartment," he explained, chuckling. "I own the building and lease the shop." He took her suitcase and led her round to the side where the stairs led up to a surprisingly spacious porch. He opened the door to his apartment, and Karen was even more surprised at how large it was.

"Come through," he invited her, and after he closed the door, he led her back to the second bedroom where he deposited her suitcase and turned to her. "Welcome to my home!" he said and kissed her.

She rested her hands on his chest, and he held her closer, wrapping his own around her, spreading his hands downward to rest on her bottom and pulling her in to his hardening body.

"I've been missing you, baby!"

His words, and the husky tone of his voice shattered her control, and she threw her arms around him, hugging him tightly. "Me too, love!"

They stood there, lost in the taste and scent and feel of each other, oblivious to all but their lust and need. His tongue found hers and suckled there hungrily. Her hands found his back and stroked him. He pushed his hips against hers, and she pushed back.

"I should get you some lunch," he murmured, though he made no move to leave. Instead, he nibbled on her earlobe and sipped from her lips again.

"I'll help you," she offered between kisses, "if you'll let me up for air!"

He heard the amusement in her voice and chuckled, slowly letting her go. "Come on then! I know I've been greedy, but I can wait a bit longer. You're here now!"

Taking her hand, he led her out, showing her his bedroom, the bathroom, the living room and dining room, then took her to the kitchen where Scrooge was curled up asleep by the door.

"I'll introduce you when he wakes up," he said, squeezing her hand. "Now, just sit there and let me get organized. Lunch will be ready in a jiffy!" He bent to kiss her once more, then turned away to busy himself with lunch.

Karen watched Peter move around his kitchen expertly, and she thought, not for the first time, how much there still was to know about him. He was a widower, but other than that and the job he did, she knew nothing about his life. And yet here she was, sitting at his kitchen table, completely at ease. Her safety radar was asleep, and if she were to be completely honest, had never once tripped with him. The thought that she was safe made the last walls crumble inside her, and suddenly she was overwhelmed with emotion as she watched his big hand wield the knife, his broad shoulders filling the fridge as he bent to take out cheese and sandwich meats. She tore her eyes away from the sight of his broad back and long legs and forced her mind to think of things other than what those legs might look like without the screen of clothing. She knew he rode his bicycle most places, so she assumed they would be muscular. The thought of those muscular legs between her own had her almost leaping out of the chair to pace away to the window farthest from where he worked.

Her sudden movement seemed to startle the dog, who cracked an eye open and stared at her in a Cyclops-like fashion. She stared back, immobilized by discomfort. For some reason she didn't understand, she felt cautious rather than afraid of what she could see was a big dog. A Labrador, if she wasn't mistaken. The dog opened the other eye, still with his head on his paws, and continued to watch her, unmoving, unblinking. Karen wondered what his name was, but just as she was about to ask, he stood up, shook himself lazily and strolled over to her to sniff her.

Peter turned around immediately, and said, "Shake, Scrooge!"

Karen felt a warm pad on her hand and looked down to see the dog waiting for her to shake his paw. Surprised and inordinately amused, she laughed softly and shook "hands" with him, then watched him walk over to his master and butt him gently in the leg, as if to ask, *who's she?*

"Your dog's name is Scrooge?" she asked, amusement still thrumming through her, mixed with relief that the animal seemed to be quite tame.

"Yes," Peter answered, chuckling softly as he put things on the kitchen table. "Come on, let's have lunch!" he continued, gesturing for her to take a seat while he retrieved a bottle of wine and two glasses. "Please help yourself!" he invited her as he poured the wine.

Karen took a sandwich and placed it on her plate and took a sip of wine. Up close, she could smell the cologne he used, a tangy, spicy flavor that married itself to the scent of the man who wore it. Even that was turning her on, and she hastened to give herself something safe to think about.

"So, why Scrooge?" she asked, taking a bite of her own sandwich.

"It's an acronym, based on a note left with him at the pound," Peter explained. "'Sorry, can't raise one more goddamned pet,' it said. The m and the p didn't fit for the acronym, so they added the o and e to finish the word."

"It's a very clever name. Did you come up with that?" she wanted to know, amused.

"No, they did," he said, "and since it seemed to describe his past owner so well, I let it stay."

"When did you first get him?" she asked.

Peter gave her a look which told her he knew what she was doing. It was knowing and amused and aroused all at once. But he answered her question anyway.

"He was about two months old," he said, "and I couldn't resist him."

Karen eyed the big dog. "I wonder how he would get on with a cat," she mused.

"When I travel, I leave him with a friend who has a house full of cats," he explained. "Her cats all love Scrooge, and he seems to love them right back." He paused, watching her finish her sandwich. "Do you have a cat?" he asked her.

"Not now, no," she said. "But I had two back in the States. I had to give them up for adoption when I moved here."

She tried to hide the sadness she felt at that, partly because she didn't want to get maudlin over them, and partly because she thought it was a sign of weakness on her part to become so emotional over a couple of felines.

"What were their names?" he asked gently.

"Bones and Spruce," she answered at once. "Both male, one all skin and bones when I found him, the other with fur that was two-colored, like the blue spruce in my yard." She sighed. "I do miss them."

A simple statement that gave away a lot about her. She hurried on. "Anyway, I can't think about pets till I have established my own place of residence, now can I?" she asked on a forced laugh.

"No, I suppose that wouldn't be wise," Peter answered, pouring a second glass of wine for her.

"Drink up!" he ordered and smiled when she complied at once.

A companionable silence followed during which they polished off the sandwiches he had made, then Scrooge got up to sniff her again. Karen bore his attention with less tension this time, though she still stiffened for a moment before she relaxed and bent over to scratch him behind the ears. The dog sniffed her face, and before she could move away, he licked her from chin to forehead, thankfully on the side, so his warm tongue missed her mouth. A bubble of laughter, a bit hysterical, burst from her lips, but she bore the doggy kiss with more equanimity than she would have thought possible before and even managed to scratch behind his ears before Peter called him off.

"I see you've made a second conquest in this house," he commented, his low tone sounding seductive to her. "Not surprising, really, given who you are. Scrooge likes women, but he has never, in all the time I've had him, kissed any of them, till now."

Karen's head shot up, and the question was out of her mouth before she could censor it. "He likes women? You've had many of them here, then?"

The second the question was spoken, she clapped her hands over her mouth in horror and felt the blood rush beneath her cheeks.

"I'm sorry! That's none of my business, Peter. Please forgive me!"

She was not a shy woman, but her reserve would not normally have let her ask such a personal and inquisitive question. She, above all, understood other people's need for personal space, for privacy, for secrets no one else should know. And she had just broken a cardinal rule of personal behavior and intruded with an impertinent question. She didn't notice that he had moved because she had closed her eyes in embarrassment, so when she heard his voice over her shoulder, she started in surprise.

"If your question means what I'd like it to mean, then I don't mind it at all."

Karen turned slowly and stood up, noting the look of desire and love in his eyes. "And what do you want it to mean?" she asked, regaining her composure.

He smiled, a gleam in his eyes. "If it means you're jealous, that's a good thing in my mind." He stepped closer, not touching her but definitely invading her personal space. "Are you?"

"Jealousy is a sign of insecurity, immaturity, and lack of trust," Karen answered, stalling. "I'm neither weak nor insecure." She slid her gaze away from his.

He brought it back with a finger under her chin. "No, you're not," he agreed. "But what of trust?" he wondered. "Do you trust me, Karen?"

She did not answer at once but stared back at him, her eyes taking in his strong, masculine features, his blue eyes now darkened with emotion, his lips that begged to be consumed. He stood silently before her, bearing her unwavering scrutiny, waiting for her answer. She could not tell from his stare what he was feeling.

"Yes, Peter, I trust you," she finally replied.

He inhaled deeply before responding. "Then in the interests of full disclosure, because I want to keep that trust, let me say I have not brought any other woman here. Just you. The women Scrooge has met have all been family or longtime friends from before Alijd died or women in the park."

He reached out a hand that she noted was trembling slightly and cupped the cheek his dog had licked earlier. "And now he has met you." He smiled into her eyes, before stepping closer until their bodies touched. "And I think he has given you his seal of approval, don't you?"

Karen relaxed, smiling at him, and nodded as he lowered his head to invade her mouth with his tongue. No gentle preamble here, no mincing steps, but a full-frontal assault that breached the walls of her reserve, that shredded her control, that consumed her. She tasted the wine on his tongue, and the unique flavor that was him. He pulled her into his arms, and she went willingly, raising her own to hug him as they kissed each other with a growing fire of passion. His body was hot and hard, and her own caught fire from the intense, burning flames that seemed to leap between them. He slid his hands down her back to her bottom and pulled her into his thighs, testing her, waiting to see what she would do.

She felt the hard press of his arousal like a searing iron on her mound, and she widened her stance to give him better access to the center of her heat. He pressed in further, squeezing and kneading the fleshy mounds he held in his hands, groaning when she circled her hips in response to his seduction.

"It's been a very long time for me, Karen," he whispered raggedly when he released her mouth to catch a breath, "so I'll need you to be patient with me while I get my groove back!"

She chuckled at the twinkle in his eyes and said, "I never would have thought you'd know that phrase! But I promise to assist with that project and bring you back up to speed quickly."

They enjoyed the intimacy of their teasing, licking each other's lips, nipping at each other, and Karen leaned her head to the side to give him better access to her neck when she saw he needed it. She felt him sucking her and wondered vaguely if he was marking her. She didn't think he would leave a hickey where anyone but they would see it, and she let him have his way. She licked him behind the ear, and when he hissed, she smiled, and repeated the action, glad to have found a sweet spot in such an unlikely place.

"You're playing with fire, you know," he murmured and bit her earlobe. When she moaned, he bit the other one, then licked it to soothe the tiny ache he'd caused. "And I fully intend to burn you up in it!"

His voice was rough with lust, making her knees buckle. He held her up, kissing her hungrily, deeply, dragging her body hard against his own.

"Come," he demanded at last, a man at the end of his control. "Before I ravish you in my kitchen!"

CHAPTER 15

Peter led Karen to his bedroom and backed her onto the wide bed, falling on top of her and pressing her into the mattress. She moaned when he ground his erection into the space she immediately opened between her thighs.

"How long has it been for you, hmm?" he whispered. "Are you as desperate as I am?"

"Yes!" was all she could manage as he kissed his way down her body, removing clothing as he did. He suckled her naked breasts, feasting on the heavy mounds of flesh, raising her nipples to turgid peaks, licking them and drawing moans of pleasure from her. Pushing her jeans and panties down her legs, he bared her sex to his gaze and lowered his head to sniff her, much like his dog had done earlier.

"You smell like heaven, baby!" he said, and licked her.

Karen arched off the bed at the unexpected contact, then was powerless to stop the assault on her senses brought on by his tongue on her clitoris and in her soaking vagina. He ate at her greedily, like a starving man at a feast, and when he pushed in one finger, then two, then three into her core, and suckled the sensitive little bundle of nerves at the top of her cleft, she convulsed around him, utterly undone by the rush of sensation. Her mouth opened but no sound came out, only short, harsh breaths as he wrung the last spasm of pleasure from her.

"Mmmmm!" His moan of pleasure vibrated against her sensitive bud, and she gasped and pulled his head away.

"Peter, please!" she implored him, begging for time to adjust to the new demands being made on her body. It had been too long since she had been touched by anything other than a rubber dick and her own fingers, and the thought of whose fingers and mouth had just brought her to her first partner-induced orgasm in a while drove her crazy with renewed desire.

"Whatever you want, my love," he promised and kissed her wet lips deeply before rising to shuck his clothing. Before her breathing had returned to normal, he was naked. Karen's mouth dropped open in shock and lust when she saw his magnificent erection standing proudly out from his body. She salivated as she wondered what it would feel like to have the steel rod he displayed for her hungry eyes inside her. She'd had enough sex before to have a fair idea of what a man's endowments could look like, and his were seriously impressive.

"I have wanted you for a very long time," he said, sheathing his cock and crawling back over her, letting his shaft rest in the welcoming nest of her pubic curls. "I dream of you and wake up wet and aching." He smoothed her hair back from her forehead, kissing her hungrily over and over, feasting on her before releasing her to add, "Now, you're mine. Can anything be better than this?"

He rubbed himself against her, and they both groaned, returning time and again to each other's mouths before he raised himself and pushed into her with one hard thrust. She cried out, a breath away from a second orgasm, and he pulled out slowly, prolonging the agony of pleasure for her.

"Shall I take you softly, like this?" he whispered, slowly sliding his shaft back inside her hungry sex. She whimpered and shook her head no. "Like this, then?" he continued, teasing her with a deep, long thrust. She gasped and clung to his shoulders, raising her legs to show him what she wanted. "Maybe like this, then!" he concluded, withdrawing and slamming back home.

They grunted as their hips met in violent surrender to the other's desires, and they fucked each other madly. All control was lost as she raised her hips to slam into him, her ravenous depths swallowing his rigid cock, his thrusts hard and deep, their flesh slapping together in rhythmic crests of sound and feeling. When she urged him to go faster and deeper, he raised himself on his hands and obliged her, slamming into her with a violence that stunned her as it pleased her.

"Oh god, yes!" she wailed as she felt her body bow before the absolute command in his hips. She rocked up into him, and when he cried out in pleasure and stiffened above her, his mouth open in ecstasy, she came again, washing them both in her juices, milking his shaft that she could feel pulsing and spasming inside her. She met each final, sharp jerk of his body until they were spent, and he sank down on top of her, his breath coming in hard gasps into the side of her neck.

They lay there, legs tangled together, catching their breath, then he rolled to the side and removed the condom before pulling her with him and settling her spine against his hairy chest.

"Are you alright?" he asked, kissing her shoulder.

"Oh yes!" she replied, a smile of deep satisfaction lighting her features. "Very alright!" She turned her head to look at him, and added, "Are you?"

He smiled tenderly at her and nodded, his eyes searching hers to find something she could not name. "Very alright, *liefje!*" he said, echoing her answer. He dropped another butterfly kiss on her cheek and turned her fully to face him, his arms surrounding her.

"This wasn't too soon?" he asked, the worry plain now on his face. "I didn't rush you?"

Karen smiled and smoothed the frown from his brow. "No, you were very restrained, love," she whispered, reaching up to kiss his lips.

Peter kissed her back slowly, savoring the taste of her, loving the way her body fit under his when he rolled back on top of her, loving the way she made him harden again with her caresses and the look in her eyes. It had been so long that he had thought he would lose control before he had had time to give her pleasure, but he knew now that even had he lost it, he would have been able to redeem himself because here he was, ready as ever again.

He pressed his hips against her, letting her feel his aching rod between her thighs, and he growled when she pushed back against him, opening and raising her legs to slide him back inside. He was not a vulgar man by nature, but her wet heat, the smell of her arousal, and her moans of pleasure at the feel of him inside made him want to swear to relieve the feelings swamping him.

"I didn't mean to ..." he began, not wanting her to think him insatiable, even if he was just then.

"I did!" She cut him off, nipping his bottom lip and pushing up against him, taking him deeper into her body. "If you want to, we can stay here for the rest of the day!"

She winked at him as she spoke and licked his bottom lip, and Peter was lost. There was no way to regain even a semblance of the composure he strove for at all times because this woman stripped him bare in no time. He began to move, at first in slow and steady strokes, adjusting his body so he could hit her g-spot with every stroke. Her gasps and hisses of pleasure told him he was doing it right, and it made him hard as a spike. He wondered as he moved faster if he would ever lose the erection that he was using even now to spear her to her heart. And then, when she raised her legs to take him deeper, he forgot to wonder about anything. He almost forgot to breathe. He pounded her flesh, taking her over and over, kissing her hungrily as he staked his claim in her willing heat, feeling her open wide and grip him with her inner walls and her heels against his buttocks.

"*Ik hou van je, liefje!*" he whispered as he loved her, trailing kisses from her cheeks down to her breasts where he stopped to suckle as he fucked her. He could feel her tightening around him, getting ready to explode again, and he adjusted his hips to rub his cock against that spot that would make her go off like firecrackers. When she howled in his arms, he let himself go and came right behind her, pumping his seed into her.

They shuddered together, spent and sated, and Peter rolled with her again until they were on their sides facing each other. But this time, his lust having been sated, he remembered that he had not worn a condom. Horror and shame gripped him, and when their breathing returned to normal, he stroked the hair back from her face, a fierce frown on his own.

"I didn't protect you, love!"

He stopped abruptly, unable to continue speaking. The thought of his carelessness was more than he could bear. He knew he was healthy, and he trusted Karen to be healthy, too, but she was still young enough to bear children, and he didn't want to impose on her in that way. They hadn't talked about anything permanent, and a baby was a very permanent thing between a couple.

"Protect me?" she asked, furrowing her own brow in confusion. "I trust you, Peter, and I'm clean."

"Yes, but what about children?" He was genuinely horrified, not because he wouldn't be over the moon if he had children after all this time, but because he didn't know Karen's feelings on the matter, and he'd rather have her than kids.

"No worries, Peter," she said with a smile. "I protect myself. Always have done. It's my body, so it's my responsibility." After a short pause, she added, "Are you relieved?"

Peter stared at her for a few seconds, then answered, "Not for the reason you think." He bent to kiss her before ending with, "If it were something we had discussed and agreed on, I'd be thrilled."

After a time, Karen spoke again. "Peter, what did that mean? What you said to me?" she asked.

"What?" Peter asked, unsure of what she was asking

"When we were making love, you said '*Ig how fan ... something*'."

"*Ik hou van je, liefje?*" he asked with a smile.

"Yes! That's it."

"It means 'I love you, darling'!" he answered, smoothing her hair.

"I love you, too," she mumbled back.

He watched her nuzzle his hand, then snuggle up to him. He smiled, knowing she must be a bit tired from the traveling. Her breathing deepened, and he pulled her body to his, ignoring the wet spot, letting her doze. The long shadows of late afternoon draped the room in gray and butter cream, and when she stirred at last, the gray had won.

"I'm sorry. Did I fall asleep?" she asked, abashed.

"I must have worn you out," he said facetiously to raise a laugh. He succeeded, and she forgot to be embarrassed. "Time for a shower, love. And then you can come with me when I walk Scrooge. You'll get to see a bit of my neighborhood."

Karen readily agreed, and though he knew she was surprised that he let her shower alone, she was quickly dressed and ready again. He joined her soon after and whistled for the dog. He took her along the usual path he followed, past the stores down the side streets that led to the park. He let the dog off his leash and let him run, watching him play and answering her questions.

"Don't you need to clean up after him?" she wanted to know.

"Yes, but Scrooge has his special spot. Whenever he's had enough and heads over there, I know it's time for cleaning duty."

He watched her face as she took in the quiet night scenery. The light from a streetlamp illuminated her face, casting it in shadow-light, lending her an air of mystery. There were many things he did not know about her, and he hoped this week with her would give him some answers. But he knew in his gut that she was his, that they belonged together, and he was confident that any issues that arose they would deal with together. She was that kind of woman—his kind.

"Tomorrow we'll drive to the music festival, and afterward, I'll take you out for a bite of supper. Sound too much?" He waited for her to answer him, then added, "I think you'll like the concert. They have an eclectic mix of music."

"How far away is it?" Karen asked.

"Almost two hours, but there will be lots to see. And after supper, we'll stay the night and drive back the day after." He hoped she wouldn't mind, but he wanted her to rest as well as enjoy herself.

"That sounds quite pleasant," she replied, smiling at him.

Peter turned when he heard Scrooge bark, and they watched the dog playing with another rather large animal whose owner looked on indulgently. The woman was very tall, strikingly blonde and, even in the dim light, clearly very beautiful. Karen felt immediately dowdy as she allowed herself to be escorted over to where the dogs played.

"Good evening, Elke. How are you?" Peter smiled at the woman, who smiled back widely, and reached over to hug him. Karen bit the inside of her cheek, remembering the conversation they had had earlier about jealousy. *I am not jealous,* she told herself and schooled her features into a smile when Peter introduced them to each other.

"Elke, please meet my friend Karen Mullings. Karen, Elke de Graaf."

"It's so nice to meet you," Elke said, her manner friendly. "Peter and I have known each other since his wife's illness, and I look after Scrooge when he's away."

Karen murmured something wholly unintelligible but kept the smile plastered on her face as she shook hands with the woman she wanted to dislike but found she couldn't. Elke's smile was open, her eyes speculative as she looked between Karen and Peter.

"So, how long are you here for?" she wanted to know. "It would be nice to have you both over for dinner, and you could meet Remi and the twins. And it would give us a chance to catch up with you, Peter!"

"I'm here for a week," Karen answered, wondering who Remi was and hoping he was a husband, and that Elke was the mother of twins. "Peter invited me to accompany him to the Africa music festival."

Elke grinned. "Oh yes, we've been with him, too, and it was such fun! I'm sure you'll enjoy it!" She turned and whistled for her dog before adding, "I'd better be getting back now. We have guests coming over for drinks, and Remi isn't home as yet. I'll call you next week, Peter, and we'll make arrangements for dinner together before Karen leaves. Nice to meet you, Karen."

Karen watched her attach the leash to her dog, aware that Peter had moved away from her side.

She waved back at the beautiful goddess who was Peter's friend and dog watcher and turned to see Peter cleaning up after Scrooge. He put the dog back on his leash, and as they walked back to his apartment, she asked about Elke.

"We met through family years ago. Remi is a distant cousin of Alijd's. They've been married for a few years. The twins are Remi's from a first marriage. His first wife also died, and they were a great comfort to me when Alijd passed."

"Is he much older than her?" Karen asked.

"By about ten years or so, yes. They are very compatible and very happy together, though. You'll like Remi and the children."

When they got back, Peter fed and watered the dog and set about making dinner. Karen offered to help, but he refused, inviting her instead to go and choose some music for them to listen to as they ate. He told her where the player was, where the CDs were, and how to use the remote control. She noted the piano, which looked as though it were used often, as well as the violin, and wondered how well he played each instrument. Turning her attention to the racks with CDs neatly stacked on them, she browsed until she found music with which she was familiar. Armik's guitar playing made everything seem more intimate and sensual, and she was in the mood for that. She pressed Play and went back to the kitchen.

Peter looked up as she walked in. "I like your taste in music," he commented with a grin. "He's one of my favorite guitarists."

"Let me at least lay the table for you," she offered.

"The placemats and utensils are over there," he said, pointing to a set of drawers next to the stove. "Plates and glasses are directly above."

Before long, they were enjoying the quiche and salad he had prepared, though he was quick to admit that the quiche was store bought. The food was good and filling, and the wine an excellent complement to it. He refused to let her help with the dishes, but soon they were sitting side by side on the couch, listening to the music and cuddling.

Karen let contentment slide over and through her, smiling at the way she felt in the arms of this man. His kisses went from soft and cherishing to hard and wanting to deep and lustful to wild and uncontrolled. And Karen went wherever he led her, giving in to the desires she had for so long suppressed so she could live in some kind of peace. Now she felt at peace, and when he pulled her to her feet and took her back to his bed, she clung to him as though he were her lifeline.

"I want you, baby!" he whispered passionately as he began to strip away her clothing. "I don't think I'll ever get enough of you!"

Karen's heart raced, her breath shallowing under his tongue as he bent to suckle on the breast he had just exposed. She mewled when he licked her between her breasts, then took a leisurely tour around one breast with his tongue whilst exploring the other with his hand. When he switched sides and slid a hand down her front to her already very wet heat, she groaned and reached for his erection, intent on pleasuring him as he was her. She gripped him through his slacks and squeezed, making him groan against her breast.

Peter stood away from her and stripped off his clothes quickly, and Karen ate him up with her eyes, reaching for his hardness as soon as he loomed over her again.

"You're so beautiful," she said, smiling at him.

Peter chuckled. "I think that's my line, isn't it?"

He reached down to fondle her where she was wet and hungry for him as he kissed her deeply, swallowing the words she was saying in response. She rode the fingers he thrust into her, widening her legs so he could penetrate her deeply. It felt so good, she could barely think, and she struggled to keep stroking his hard cock. His fingers were big and long and filled her, and he stroked her sweet spot with every pass, making her grow hot with hunger, pleasure sizzling through her, zapping her nerves and sparking tingles in her fingertips and toes. When he added his mouth on her breast, suckling strongly, she lost all ability to think and simply let herself feel as he drove her over the top and into freefall. She cried out, her legs shaking, her heart thudding so hard she felt it might leap out of her chest, her arms too weak to do more than fall limply at her side.

She was still gasping from the orgasm when he thrust into her hard, his hips slapping against hers loudly, his grunts of pleasure fueling the embers still burning in the core of her being. Karen could feel the steel hardness of him sliding in and out of her wet sheath, and the agonizing pleasure of its touch against her g-spot with every inward thrust. She raised her legs and thrust her hips to meet his, wanting to be one with him, to melt into his flesh and bones, to share the strength of her passion with him in every way.

"Oh darling, you feel so good!" he said hoarsely. "You're like warm silk, sucking me in, swallowing me. Don't let me go, baby!"

Karen squeezed him with her inner walls, a silent promise to obey him. She twisted her hips when he thrust in, wringing another groan from him. He sped up, and she kept time with his thrusts, wrapping her arms around his neck and enjoying the feeling of him riding her hard. His body glistened with sweat, and his warm breath caressed her face as he took her. The heat rose between them, their breathing becoming more and more labored as they loved each other. Fire raced through her, and Karen let herself be consumed in the flames, needing to fall again in his arms.

"Peter, please ..."

Her whispered plea echoed between them with lust and longing, and Peter looked into her eyes, and she saw when he let go. A second later, she felt the gush of his semen inside her, and she fell off the edge again with him. Her scream of ful-fillment was silent because the joy was too great, the pleasure too intense, the ecstasy too much.

Peter's roar said it for the two of them, and Karen heard it through the fog of her own escalating ful- fillment. She saw stars—apparently that wasn't a cliché!—and they blinded her for long moments while she shuddered and pulsed.

She felt the weight of her lover's body leave her, and she moaned a protest until he spooned in behind her, pulling her against his chest and hugging her tightly to him, kissing her damp shoulders and her hair, whispering softly to her until she fell asleep. What felt like a very short time later, she was awakened by a hungry mouth on her breasts, and a hard thigh between hers, one hand caressing her little button, stoking the fire that had only dimmed but not gone out after they were last together. She raised her leg and gave him greater access, and Peter took the hint, sending his fingers up into her core, readying her for that other more intimate invasion. Their love- making this time was slow and languorous, tender and full of love. Peter's kisses, when he rolled her to her back and slid into her, were deep and rav- enous, but his hands were gentle upon her, his thrusts slow and powerful, as though he meant to get to the very heart of her. When they climaxed, Karen a breath after Peter, she clung to him, let- ting the love that was growing inside her bloom and fill her.

CHAPTER 16

"Darling, we need to get going. It's a longish drive, and we don't want to miss any of the concert."

His words wafted over her cheeks as he peppered her face with soft brushes of his lips. He avoided her mouth, and she could well imagine that that might be deliberate as they both knew to kiss her there would mean they'd not leave the bed for a few more hours yet. She let him pull her up, and they showered together, managing to keep their desires under control. After dressing, Karen in her room, they had a quick breakfast while Peter called Elke and asked her to walk Scrooge that evening as he would be away for the night. They took their overnight bags out to the car and were soon off.

Apparently, Karen was more tired than she had realized because the next time she opened her eyes, Peter was pulling into the parking area.

"Welcome back!" he said, smiling at her flushed cheeks. "You had a nice doze, love, and you're just in time for the show!"

They got in easily as Peter had already bought the tickets, and they settled into their seats. Just before the concert began, her cell phone rang. She took it out, but before she turned it off, she checked to see who was calling. It was Toni, and she answered quickly, raising her voice to be heard above the noise of the crowd. "Toni! What a lovely surprise! How are you, sweetie?"

"I'm good, thanks! So glad I caught you. Just wanted to let you know Niall and I are traveling and will be in Amsterdam on Tuesday. We wondered if you might like to meet us, with Peter, for lunch?"

The first band was being introduced, so Karen said hurriedly, "I'll let you know by the end of the day, okay? Have to run now. The show's about to start. Bye!"

She rang off and sat back, letting Peter's arm encircle her shoulders. She felt warm and treasured and relaxed against him when he pulled her into his side. He squeezed her shoulders, and she felt him drop a kiss on the top of her head.

"You'll like this band," he announced as they struck a chord and began.

Karen settled back to enjoy herself, happy to let Peter be her musical guide. There were no worries, and all was right with the world. The concert that day was thrilling to Karen, who had never heard so much African music all at once and who found the blends of rhythms and sounds delightfully exotic. She forgot where she was and simply basked in the music. When it was over, she could still feel the drumbeats in her hands as though she had played them, and she could hear the bass voices blending with the others in perfect harmony ringing through her ears and resounding in the spaces around her.

"That was brilliant!" she enthused as Peter walked her to a local eatery for dinner. The food was plain fare, but delicious, and perhaps it was a suitable counterpoint to the richness of the music she had just enjoyed. And she basked in the warmth of her lover's regard, seeing in his eyes when they rested on her a depth of feeling and hunger that she had never expected ever to see in a man's eyes for her, though she had hoped.

"I had a really lovely day, Peter!" she said as they shared a decadent double-sized banana split. "Thank you for inviting me."

His smile warmed every corner of her being, and his words only enhanced the feeling. "You're welcome, *liefje*! I did, too. I don't think I have ever enjoyed a concert as much in a very long time." He reached for her hand as he spoke, squeezing her fingers gently. "Would you like to stay one more night and hear the rest tomorrow?"

"Sure, if it's all right with you," she replied, "but what about Scrooge?"

"It's no problem to ask Elke to watch him one extra night for me. I'll do it now."

She listened idly as he made the arrangements, and as it occurred to her to wonder where they would sleep for the extra night, he said, "I made a reservation for two nights, on the off chance that you might like to stay."

She chuckled, amused at the sly look on his face as he spoke. "I'll decide later whether to be concerned that you have a sneaky side or not," she announced, trying to sound severe and failing.

His laughter filled the space between them, low and surprisingly sexy. He was like a man half his years, and she felt a powerful surge of pride that she had been the one, after all this time, to bring his heart back to life. She loved the way he spoke, the way he pronounced English words, the way he called her "darling" in his language, the way he touched her with fire and reverence. She wondered how she had managed to become so connected to him after only a few months, most of them spent with him online or on the phone.

"A penny for your thoughts?" His voice interrupted her musings, and she smiled again, suddenly deliriously happy.

"I was thinking about you," she said, blushing faintly.

"And what, in particular, were you thinking?" he wanted to know.

She hesitated a breath, then answered his curiosity. "I was thinking how I like your accent and the way you pronounce English words." *Better some truth than a lie,* she thought.

"And here I was hoping you might perhaps be thinking of what we shared last night, and again this morning, and hoping we could do it again."

The faint pink in her cheeks bloomed under the suggestive sultriness of his words and the look she caught in his eyes before he turned to summon a waiter. A fine trembling began in her fingers, and she clasped her hands together in her lap to stop the movement. She could not remember ever having been so thoroughly seduced before this man and this moment, despite the men she had had in her life. She watched him pay for their meal and took the hand he held out to her as they walked out into the evening air. They drove sedately to the small bed and breakfast he had booked their room in, though she knew he was feeling the urgency of their shared desire beating against him as it was against her.

The room, at any other time, would have elicited delighted commentary from her, but she was beyond noticing anything other than the man whose arms wrapped her in heat and hunger, whose tongue demanded and received entry into her desirous mouth, whose leg pushed between her own, and settled her core over its rock hardness, allowing her to set herself aflame as he helped her ride his thigh. The vivid blue curtains that twinkled with a firmament of silk escaped her notice; the jeweled beauty of the matching bed coverings onto which he lowered her disappeared beneath the weight of his heated gaze. The warm yellow lamplight that he had dimmed was nothing to the blazing light of love and lust that illuminated the space between her eyes and his.

"I cannot begin to explain to you how very deeply you affect me, *liefje*. The last time I felt this out of control around a woman, I was barely out of my teens." His whispered words sank into her bones, into her very soul, as he kissed her again and finished what he began with those first kisses by the door.

Afterward, as they lay panting in each other's arms, Karen wondered where their new relationship would end up. Neither of them had spoken of anything beyond their feelings for each other. And she was old enough, and cynical enough, to know that just because he wanted her body and couldn't seem to get enough of it didn't mean he wanted a firmer commitment to her. He had been married once, and by all accounts, it had not been a happy marriage at the end. She wasn't sure she could blame him if he chose not to pursue anything further with her. She knew it would hurt her to have given her heart to someone who didn't want more, but she would not press him or even let a hint of her worries show. She would let him decide on his own.

She fell asleep in his arms, and when morning brightened the room in the blue glow of the curtains, she woke to find herself alone in bed. Peter was standing by the bathroom door, speaking softly into his cell phone. She wondered who had called so early, but when she looked at her own device, it showed that she had been asleep for almost nine hours. She sat up and stretched as he finished his call and walked back to the bed.

"Did you sleep well?" he asked, smiling warmly at her.

"Yes, I did," she replied. "And for far longer than usual. It's almost eight o'clock."

She watched him look up in surprise, and she explained, "I don't normally get as much as six hours of sleep a night. I just can't seem to stay in bed long enough. My body starts to hurt, and the muscles feel strained, and I have to get up. So, nine hours is a very long time!"

He reached over and kissed her gently on the lips. "Well, I'm glad you were able to catch up on some sleep, then, love." He stood again, and said, over his shoulder, "Shall I order breakfast in bed for you?"

Karen chuckled. "No, of course not! I'd rather we eat out and then go back to listen to some more of that lovely music!"

"It'll be different artists today, and the concerts end in the early afternoon."

"Let's hurry then, shall we?"

She hopped out of bed, and only once her feet touched the carpet did she remember she was naked, never having had a chance to put on the pretty nightie she had packed for the trip. It was too late to be modest now, but she could not stop the suffusion of heat that warmed her skin all over as she walked past him to the bathroom. Once inside, behind the closed door, she exhaled and wondered when she would get over being embarrassed to be naked with him. She excused herself because they had only been lovers for two days, after all, and this would take some getting used to.

A hot shower behind her, she wrapped herself in a towel and returned to the bedroom to find Peter sitting in an armchair, obviously waiting his turn. He put down the magazine he was thumbing through when she announced, "All yours!" and rose to have his own shower. She hoped there would be enough hot water for him. By the time he came out, drying his hair with another towel, brown slacks riding low on his hips where they settled, zipped up halfway, she was putting on light makeup. Her eyes caught the trail of hair, some silver, that snaked down inside his pants, and she dragged them away before she got entangled in thoughts of what they had shared for the last two days. She didn't want to make more of it than he did, though she did see him go hard, as though he felt her eyes on him.

She turned back to apply mascara, but finding her hand was trembling a bit too much, she decided to go back to powdering her cheeks until her nerves were steady enough. Eventually, she felt presentable and turned to find him right behind her, his button-down shirt tucked into his pants, his belt buckled, the signs of a waning erection still evident behind his zipper. She raised her eyes to his face and saw the hunger he did not try to hide from her shooting from the depths of his own, but before she could utter a word, he was on her, his mouth consuming hers, his hands kneading the muscles of her shoulders before sliding in a tenacious grip down her arms to her back, thence to her bottom, where he massaged her as he pulled her in to his body.

"Are you hungry?" he wanted to know, his voice low and rusty. He nipped her earlobe as he waited for her to respond.

Karen cleared her throat, which was suddenly clogged, but even then could only manage a weak, "Yes," hoping he would think she meant for food and not for the thrust of his body inside her own.

"So am I, *meisje*," he said, licking the pulse that beat in her throat, trailing his lips up to the one that beat in her temple and kissing her there, leaving her in no doubt as to the kind of hunger of which he spoke. "So am I." He trailed his tongue back over her throat, suckling the vein there lightly, then raised his head and inhaled deeply. "But I can wait. Let's go have breakfast. The concert will begin at ten today."

He stepped away from her then, which gave her the room to move and the time to recoup her lost composure and gather her scattered wits along with her pocketbook. He took her arm and escorted her from the room, out to a full breakfast in the large country kitchen of the house, before they went for a second day to listen to songs and stories and wander booths of artwork. Before she knew it, the concert was over, and Peter was leading her away from the stall where she had purchased a wooden carving of lovers just about to kiss. She fancied she could feel the warm breath passing between their lips, and she smiled as she thought of where she could put it in her house, if she had one.

"What are you thinking?" Peter's voice brought her sharply back to the moment, and to the sidewalk down which they were strolling.

"Just wondering where an item like the carving I bought could be placed in a house I might someday own," she answered. It struck her, as she said it, that he might think she was angling for some kind of statement from him, and as she knew that was not her intention, she hurried on without letting him speak. "Anyway, Toni and Niall are in Amsterdam, and she asked if we could pop over for lunch with them." When he did not immediately respond, she added, "I know it's a long way from your home, so if you'd rather not, that's all right with me. I can see her when I get back to England."

His continued silence began to unnerve her, but just as she was about to tackle it in her usual head-on way, he turned to her and said, "That sounds like a marvelous idea, *meisje*. Unfortunately, I won't be able to join you. Something has come up that I need to attend to."

His tone was cool, almost aloof, and Karen tried not to feel hurt at what seemed like a withdrawal. Perhaps that phone call this morning was what had come up.

"It's all right, Peter. I understand. Life happens while we're having fun." Her answer sounded lame, even to her own ears, but she was determined not to let any of her inner turmoil show.

"Let's have dinner then, shall we, and plan how to get you to your friends, and me on my way."

His hand at her elbow urged her into a restaurant she hadn't noticed, and as they were seated, she debated asking him what exactly had come up that was taking him away from her before the week he had invited her to stay was halfway done. She accepted the glass of water the waiter brought and drank deeply, as though preparing herself for battle. When prompted, she placed her order and left him to choose the wine that went with their meal while she marshaled her thoughts for the conversation she did not want to have.

"You seem preoccupied." His voice, an echo of worry in it, brought her sharply back to the moment.

"I'm not," she replied, denying it without heat. "I just wondered what had come up and if it would spoil our time together."

She gave herself full marks for sounding matter-of-fact, as aloof as he had sounded earlier. She had long ago learned to disguise what she was truly feeling beneath a mask of cool reserve.

"Oh, I'm sorry. I meant to tell you before. I have a few interviews coming up shortly. I was trying to make arrangements to have them rescheduled for next week, but it's not possible. So, I'll be away from tomorrow till Wednesday, I'm afraid."

His eyes were troubled, and Karen felt gratified that he was not any more happy with the situation than she was. It wasn't as though she had anywhere she desperately needed to be, so she could lengthen her stay, but it would cost her money to change the booking to return home, and she was determined not to pass the cost of that on to him. If he wanted her to stay longer, she would pay her own way.

"You've gone again," he murmured, sipping the wine that had been brought to their table, watching her with patient eyes.

"Sorry." She changed the subject when he remained quiet. "What are you interviewing for? A new job?"

"Yes, in a university." He offered no further explanation, making her wonder if he was reluctant to discuss it. When he changed the subject, she thought her conjecture correct. "What do you think of Leeuwarden?"

She smiled. "It's a nice city, what little I've seen of it. Have you lived there long?"

"Alijd and I moved there fifteen years ago. We lived in a house before she died, but afterwards, I wasn't comfortable living there alone. I moved to the apartment, which we had owned all along as well, and now I lease the house to family."

Their salads arrived and the meal proceeded with conversation being more of the general sort, no further mention being made of either his interviews or of the city where he lived, nor of Toni's visit to Amsterdam.

After dinner, they went back to the bed and breakfast, and as they got ready for bed, he said,

"We'll go home in the morning and look for a place for you to stay in Amsterdam. I can recommend a reasonably priced place if you like. You'll be able to spend some time with your friends, and then I'll come and pick you up. I'll have to put you on the train to get there, though. Will that be all right, love?"

His voice was faintly worried, and she hastened to reassure him. "That'll be fine, Peter. Just let me know how much it costs, okay?"

"I'll take care of ..."

Karen interrupted him. "No, that's all right. I'll handle it."

His lips thinned, and she wondered if they were about to have their first not-quite-a-couple argument. She braced herself, suddenly wishing she was the sort of woman who could just let it slide.

He inhaled deeply, then said, "Why don't we go Dutch with this, too, hmm? It would make me more comfortable."

"Sure. I don't mind that." She sighed inwardly, feeling as though she had dodged a bullet. "I'll just go brush my teeth now."

The bathroom mirror was still somewhat misted, and she watched it clear as she brushed her teeth and cleaned the makeup from her face. Peter's voice calling her reminded her she was not alone, and she walked quickly back into the bedroom.

"Sorry ... had to remove the warpaint!"

He chuckled and switched off the light as she crawled into bed next to him, and he reached for her, pulling her up against his hard body.

"I thought for a second at dinner that we were going to have our first quarrel," he murmured into her hair, stroking her arms tenderly. "I'm glad we didn't, or I wouldn't feel comfortable doing this."

He left her in no doubt as to what "this" was, and by the time they fell asleep, she had been well and truly fucked harder than she had ever been before. She had been well used, and her last waking thought was that she could get accustomed to being so thoroughly loved by this man. And when his kisses woke her up a few hours later, and his hands raised her blood pressure, and his fingers opened her, and his hard rod drove into her, she was replete with pleasure.

They drove back to Leeuwarden later in the morning, and after collecting Scrooge, they went for a walk in the park. The air was balmy, and they lingered, holding hands and enjoying each other's company. Karen felt contentment sweep through her as they walked up the stairs at his apartment behind Scrooge. She could live like this.

Once Peter had booked a room for her stay in Amsterdam, and they had eaten dinner and cleared the things away, she packed an overnight bag with things for her trip and watched Peter pack for his interviews.

"Where will you be for the next few days?" she asked him as he closed his overnight bag.

"Groningen, Haarlem, and Nijmegen," he answered. "Perhaps I could join you on Wednesday evening instead after my last interview, if you wouldn't mind," he added, turning from placing it by the door to look at her. "We can leave on Thursday morning."

"I'd love that," she replied. "Toni sent me a text message to say she and Niall would be in Amsterdam for a couple of days, so I won't be on my own on Wednesday."

Peter watched her settle herself into his bed and felt his heart turn over. There was nothing he wouldn't do for this woman, and he hoped she would come to see that they could be happy together. But he had never been one to rush into action, despite his behavior with her the last few days. And with the upheaval that a change in job would bring, he wasn't sure he should be doing even what he had already done with her until things were more settled. But he worried that her seeing Niall again, a man whom he knew she liked, although she would not come between her friend and him, might still make her think twice about anything more permanent with him. He knew she enjoyed their lovemaking as much as he did, but he wasn't certain she understood that for him, loving her was everything, and that having said the words, he was committed to her.

He got into bed, feeling his body stir as he touched her warm skin, and he wrapped his arms around her, determinedly pushing all worry from his mind so that he could immerse himself in her.

She was so receptive, giving him back kiss for kiss, opening herself to his caresses, to his desires, that he hoped she might also be committing herself to him. He loved the way she moaned when he slid his hands down to knead her breasts and when he slid his fingers between the lips of her sex to play with her clitoris. He loved the way she opened her legs to accept his invasion and thrust up against him as he drove into her. She made him mindless with lust until all he could see was her eyes, and all he could feel was her heartbeat and the wet slide of her flesh cradling his. He loved her cries of ecstasy when she came, and it pushed him over the edge.

When he was able, he rose to clean them up, but by the time he returned, she was half asleep. He wiped their juices from her flesh and slid back into bed beside her, hugging her against his chest and letting himself fall into sleep. There was a lot he had to do over the next few days, but for now, he had the woman he loved in his arms, and he would savor that.

CHAPTER 17

After a quick breakfast next morning, Peter took Karen to the train and kissed her goodbye before taking himself off to Groningen for his first interview. Arriving half an hour early, he sat in the vestibule sipping the mediocre coffee put out for visitors and considered his options. He could accept the job in Groningen if it were offered because he could stay in his flat and continue to live as he had for the last fifteen years, even though it meant a longer commute. And Karen said she didn't mind Leeuwarden, though Groningen was a lovely old city as well. The program he would be teaching in was an excellent one, and he would be happy there, he was sure. But he had lived in Groningen when he and Alijd had first married, and the memories were bittersweet, at best.

Haarlem was a lovely city, old and full of history, but he was least interested in the job he had applied for there. Its proximity to Amsterdam was one of the reasons he was even considering it. Nijmegen seemed ideal. The program he would work in was well-known in Europe, and the city itself was just the right size for his tastes. It also being close to Amsterdam was a lovely bonus, and now, with his desire, for the first time since before Alijd's death, to be married again, he thought it might be better for him to move closer to Amsterdam. It felt right because it was where he had first met Karen.

His thoughts were interrupted by the summons to the interview room, where he did his best to sound interested in a job he had decided he wouldn't take if they offered it to him. At the very least, he had to be civil. Once back on the road, he made a number of stops, deciding nothing was to be gained by hesitating or procrastinating. The next time he saw Karen, he wanted to be ready, in case she decided to give him a chance to find happiness with her. He called Elke, who was delighted to hear from him, and they agreed to dinner on Friday evening at Elke's place. She declared herself eager to help him in any way she could because she had liked what little she had seen of Karen. He was relieved. He had very few friends, and it felt good to know he could count on them when he needed them. He apologized for asking for her help with Scrooge again, explaining about his interviews in the south, and she was as willing as always to keep his dog for him.

That settled, he drove to Haarlem to another friend's home and was happy to find himself just in time for dinner.

"Peter, it's good to see you!" Dirk's handshake was firm and his smile welcoming. He was himself a widower but had recently moved to Haarlem to be with the woman he would be marrying in a month's time.

"It's good to be here, my friend!" Peter followed his friend indoors and dropped his bag next to the umbrella stand where Dirk left it, leading him to the kitchen where the table was laid.

"I hope you don't mind being informal. Ilse won't be back till much later, and I'll have to pick her up at the station."

"Informal is fine, Dirk. I'm too tired anyway. It's been rather a long day for me, and I have an early start tomorrow."

They sat down to roast duck and baby potatoes with sautéed vegetables washed down with white wine. Peter told Dirk about the jobs he was looking into but said nothing about Karen. He needed to be certain of her first before letting anyone else in on the secret. And anyway, he would have to tell Jannie before anyone else.

Later that evening, after his shower, he sat composing poetry for Karen, one of which he planned to send to her before going to bed. He assumed Karen would be out with her friends, so he didn't bother to call, just sent her the poem and went to bed.

He read Karen's reply before leaving the following morning, and after arranging to return for lunch with Dirk, set off for the school. He realized that he missed her very much after only a day apart, and he was glad he would see her again later. Not even with Alijd had he felt this intimacy, this connection that he feared, if it were lost, would break him completely. He put in a favorite CD into the changer in the car and let the music soothe him as he drove. Happily, he found a parking spot close to the building. The interview was exhaustive, and at the end of it, he didn't think they would hire him. For one thing, he came with too much experience, and therefore too high a price tag. For another, he wasn't sure he had managed to conceal completely his lack of interest in the job. *Ah well,* he was not bothered by a possible rejection. Nijmegen seemed ideal to him, and he would be sure to be on his best interview form in time for the afternoon.

Lunch was with Dirk and Ilse at a local restaurant after which he returned to their home to pick up his things and ready himself for his final meeting. Accepting hugs from his friends, Peter set off for his afternoon appointment, containing his excitement at the thought that he would see Karen in a few hours' time. He needed to focus for this last interview at the university that he really wanted to work in, and thoughts of what he would do to her later would not help him there. The interview went off without a hitch, and by early evening Peter was knocking on the door to Karen's room. He had called her after the interview was over to let her know he was on his way, and his chest expanded when it opened.

Her smile drew him in, and he barely restrained himself enough to close the door before he pulled her into his kiss. She smelled like strawberries and tasted like chocolates, and he was suddenly ravenous for her.

"I missed you, *liefje*," he confessed while stripping her of the robe she was wearing. Her hair was damp, her skin cool as though she had just finished a shower. He inhaled deeply when he saw her breasts, bending his head to suckle them. She groaned when he nipped and licked her nipples, and when he drew her panties down her legs and helped her step out of them, she relaxed completely against him.

"I missed you, too!" She sighed when he renewed his assault on her erect nipples, and as soon as he stood again to kiss her lips, she wrapped her arms around him and pulled him into her naked body. His own hardened in response, and all the pent-up lust of the past day had him pulling her to the couch and losing his clothes as fast as he ever had as a younger man. The need to be with her in the most intimate way was overwhelming, and after he had brought her crashing into orgasm twice, he took his own pleasure, not being able to hold off the hunger any longer. Heart racing, gasping for breath, he collapsed over her when the last of his cum boiled up and poured into her.

Finally, he rolled off her and pulled her up into a tender kiss. "Let's shower together," he invited her.

"We'll have to hurry," she said, picking up their clothes. "I've invited Toni and Niall for drinks. I want you to meet them."

She walked away toward the bathroom, and he was glad because he needed a few seconds to process the information and decide how he felt about it. His plans did not include a second couple and certainly not one that included a man who had once been interested in her. But he was an adult, and he was determined to make her happy in every way he could. A few drinks couldn't hurt, and at least it gave him the chance to see the man who might have been a rival for her affections and finally resolve the seed of jealousy that he now admitted had never been uprooted.

They showered quickly, and though Peter knew Karen had expected more, he found himself unable to do more than bathe her tenderly and send her to dress while he washed himself. By the time he exited the bathroom, she was dressed in a short-sleeved linen dress of pale pink that stopped just above her knees. Her feet were encased in matching pumps, and she turned to him with a smile.

"Would you zip me up, please?" She turned away again, and he reached down to pull the zipper the rest of the way up. "I went shopping with Toni yesterday while Niall was in meetings and bought this outfit. Do you like it?" She turned again as she spoke and spread her arms wide.

"It's a lovely dress, *liefje*," he said, smiling back at her. "The color suits you."

"I'd better let you get dressed," she continued, turning back to apply makeup. "Don't want Toni to arrive with you *en déshabillé.*"

She chuckled at her joke, and he relaxed, glad of her teasing. He wanted to be as natural as possible when her friends arrived. By the time he slipped his feet into his loafers, Karen was ready and watching him.

"You look good," she remarked, walking over to touch his sleeve. The long-sleeved shirt he wore was dark blue and open at the collar in deference to the warm temperatures.

"Not as good as you do, I'm sure," he replied gallantly and kissed her cheek. "I assume we're having drinks in the hotel bar?"

"Yes. I told Toni and Niall to be here by six."

As if on cue, there was a quiet knock on the door. Karen went to open it while Peter inhaled deeply and waited. A flurry of activity at the open door brought his eyes to the scene, and his smile was natural and amused. The two women were hugging each other as though they had not just met the day before. He turned his eyes to the man who stood next to them, very tall and younger than he and saw a reflection of his own amusement on Niall's face. He moved forward just as the friends broke apart.

"Peter, this is Toni," Karen gestured to her friend, "and Niall. Guys, this is Peter."

Peter found himself embraced by a vivacious dark-haired beauty, shorter than Karen but just as curvy. He shook hands with Niall, who seemed very pleasant, and was clearly besotted with Toni, for which he was truly grateful. Taking the lead, he escorted them all down to the hotel bar, and they chose a table, having decided in the elevator that they would have a pub supper as well.

"So, Karen told me you took her to a concert this past weekend," Toni said as they waited for the starters to arrive. "Is this an annual event? She seemed to enjoy it a lot, and it might be something I'd like to see myself."

Happy to be able to contribute something to the conversation, Peter gave as much detail as he thought would interest them without being boring. Karen's enthusiastic interjections pleased him, and when Niall asked if they could perhaps make up a foursome next year to take in the two-day event, he blinked in surprise but recovered quickly.

"That would be fine," he replied, and nodded when Karen excused herself to the ladies' room. Toni followed along behind her, and he chuckled at Niall's question.

"Why do women visit the restroom in pairs? I've never understood it."

Peter shook his head. "Me either, to be honest. Though in this case, I think it may have something to do with us."

Niall smiled, agreeing with him. Then his face turned serious, and he looked earnestly into Peter's face. "Karen is a beautiful woman, Peter," he began. A small silence followed, as if he needed to choose his next words, and then he continued,

"The first time I met her, I was bowled over, and sure there was a reason we had met. I was quite prepared to try and pursue her until I met Toni. In the end, I was right. We did meet for a reason." When Peter did not respond, the younger man added, "If I hadn't seen the two of you in the pub, I would not have gone back the next night and found her alone. And I wouldn't have met Toni. I just wanted to say thanks."

He stuck his hand out then, and Peter shook it, relieved that the air was clear between them and hoping that they could forge a true friendship. If Karen and Toni had anything to do with it, that was a certainty. The rest of the evening was filled with pleasant conversations, laughter, and a growing bond of camaraderie. By the time the two couples said their goodnights, and the women hugged and parted, Peter was happy that he had met and been approved of by Karen's best friend and satisfied that he had nothing to fear from the man of whom he had been secretly jealous.

He made slow love to Karen that night, bringing her time and again to the peak but not letting her go over. He wanted her wild for him; he wanted to leave his stamp on her; he wanted to mark her as his. He had never experienced anything like this rampaging feeling, this wildness that was roaring through his blood, and he took her up one last time, his hands all over her, his mouth raiding hers, his cock finally plunging deep into her, taking her hard. It felt as though his hips had a mind of their own because although he tried to slow it down, he was out of all control by the time he pushed them both into an all-consuming orgasm.

He gasped and shouted as he came over and over inside her, and she held on tightly with her arms and her legs to his shaking body, raising her hips to meet his thrusts, slamming herself into him, crying out her own release. They lay gasping for breath and utterly sated, and when she turned into the cocoon of his arms, he kissed her tenderly and watched her fall asleep.

He woke before her the next morning. It was still dark, and he slid quietly out of bed to fetch her gift from his bag. The little box was covered in blue velvet, and the sparkling diamond and ruby ring winked at him. The yellow gold band was thin but sturdy, round-edged, the way he liked it. He hoped she wasn't into the fancy new-fangled wedding sets because he was what some would call "old school" about jewelry.

He stood over the bed watching her sleep, and his heart warmed. She was everything he could ever have imagined as a lover, everything he had ever wanted, and he stifled the worry that his age might make him soon come to be less than satisfactory to her. He wasn't an old man by any means, but he was closer to fifty than forty. So far, they had been in sync, and he would do everything to ensure that they could continue to enjoy each other as they had so far been doing.

She stirred, and he sat down beside her on the bed, waiting for her to open her eyes. When she did, she was immediately awake, no confusion showing in their brown depths. She smiled, and his heart beat faster.

"Good morning, *liefje*," he whispered. "Did you sleep well?"

Her smile widened, and she nodded, yawning. "Why are you up so early?" she wanted to know, looking over at the digital clock on the radio.

"I had to get something." He pulled her up to sit next to him, wrapping the bedclothes around her to keep her warm. "I bought you a gift yesterday, and I wanted to give it to you before we went back home."

"You didn't have to buy me anything, Peter," she protested, a small frown creasing her forehead. "I wasn't expecting ..."

"This is one gift I must give you, love," he cut her off. "It's tradition." At her puzzled frown, he held out the little velvet box to her. "Go on. Open it, please. I need to know if you like it."

He waited patiently while she stared at it, comprehension dawning, her eyes darting to his face and back to the box before she took it with trembling fingers and opened it. The engagement ring winked at her, and he could see, by the way her eyes widened, that she liked it. But he would ask, anyway, just to be sure.

"Do you like it, baby?" His voice was hoarse, but there wasn't much he could do about it at the moment.

"It's beautiful, Peter. Thank you!"

She looked into his eyes but did not take the ring from the box. He smiled ... how like her! He loved that she didn't jump the gun but waited for him to say his piece.

"I've felt drawn to you since the first day we met, Karen. In fact, if I were to be romantic about it, I'd say that from the start I was bowled over, pun intended. And you know how I feel about you. This was inevitable as far as I was concerned. I knew I would ask you to marry me. As I am doing now." He paused, taking both her hands in his. "I wish I knew what your answer will be. I hope it will be what I want to hear." Another pause, while he raised her hands to his lips and kissed the back of each one. "Will you marry me, *liefje*?"

She did not immediately answer him but held on to his hands. He took that as a good sign and waited, holding his breath.

"I have never told anyone else what I'm about to tell you," she began. "I've done my best to bury the memories for all these years because for me, they are a sign of my failure at relationships."

She pulled herself up to lean against the headboard, the sheets drawn up to hide her body from him. It was clear that what she was about to tell him was difficult for her to talk about.

"I have had three other marriage proposals, Peter," she said, and he tried to contain his shock. "The first was because I had gotten pregnant and his father made him propose to me. But we were both too young, too immature, and too wrong for each other. I said no, to the horror and disappointment of my parents, and the silent relief of the boy and his family. When I lost the baby, everyone but me was happy."

"How old were you?" he asked.

"We were seventeen." She looked into his eyes as if to gauge his reaction, and obviously liking what she saw, she continued. "The second time, my lover was drunk when he asked, and horrified when I told him what he had done the next day. His relief at my refusal was a slap in the face because I had begun to harbor some feelings for him ..."

Peter interrupted her. "Then why did you say no, love?"

"Because he was drunk. I wanted him to ask me when he was sober, so I would know for sure that he meant it." She sighed, and a sad smile lifted her lips for a moment. "Of course, he didn't, and I'm glad I was so sensible. Even if he did break my heart just a little bit."

"How old were you the second time?" he asked quietly.

"Thirty," she replied. "The last time was a little over a year ago." She stopped, inhaled deeply, then went on. "Jake and I had been friends for years, and when he proposed, it had seemed to be happenstance. I said yes to what I thought was a 'what if' joking proposal of marriage which I later found out had been serious. I didn't know how to back out gracefully, so I kept putting it off. Then he was killed, and I was relieved of that worry. But guilt about feeling relieved was still a heavy weight, one which I've only recently managed to let go."

"Did you love him?" Peter's voice was as still as the quiet room.

"Yes," she answered and finally looked him in the eyes. "Yes, I did. But not enough to want to live with him for the rest of my life. And not at all like I love you."

He opened his mouth to say something, but she slid a trembling finger over them, shushing him.

"This time, I'm saying yes to the right person for the right reason." She reached up and kissed him lightly on the cheek. "Yes, Peter, I will marry you."

She wiped the tear that slipped silently down his cheek as he took the ring from the box and put it on her finger. He kissed it and held her hand over his heart.

"I love you, too, Karen." When he reached for her and pulled her close, she relaxed against him. His body stirred, and he tilted her head up so he could see her eyes when he said, "You've brought me back to life when I thought I would never be alive again." He kissed her then, slowly, thoroughly, waking the need in them, and proceeded to show her how much he loved her.

EPILOGUE

Karen had always thought herself a level-headed woman until Peter put a ring on her finger. Beyonce's song kept playing over in her head ... *If you like it then you shoulda put a ring on it.* She hummed the tune as she showered, dressed, and packed her things. It rang in her head as they went down for breakfast, then checked out. It made her smile as they drove away from Amsterdam, back to Leeuwarden. It felt good to know that Peter had liked her enough to put a ring on her finger. *And oh my, what a ring!*

She tilted her hand up and spread her fingers so she could see the diamonds sparkling around the rich red ruby that went so well with her skin tone. She loved it and was so pleased that Peter was not one of those men enslaved to everything modern. Her last fiancé had been, and the ring he had given her, which she still had in the bottom of the closet she had in George's house, was a brash modern thing, platinum and white gold with stones all round its wide band. She could see about getting rid of it now.

Two months later, after they had found and bought a lovely home and had both moved into it, on a sparkling late summer afternoon, Peter and Karen said their "I do's" in a quiet, elegant ceremony attended by the very few guests they invited. Toni stood up for Karen, and Dirk for Peter. The only other guests were Dirk's new wife Ilse, Niall, Elke and Remi, Duncan and Jannie, George and Elaine. The day was warm and bright, and as they spoke their vows to each other, with smiles of sheer joy on their faces, their friends and family shared in the deep emotions they exuded.

Karen's dress was seashell white, a floor-length affair of strapless silk. She and Toni had shopped together to choose it, and after a long day of disappointing slogging from store to store, they had found it in a little shop off one of the main shopping thoroughfares in London. It shimmered with the play of light on the lace flowers interwoven with ruby-colored satin thread on the fitted bodice. The full skirt, which fell from just below her breasts, swirled when she moved, the confection of ruby-tinted chiffon drifting above the underskirt making her appear to float. The chiffon wrap that came with it would be the perfect evening covering for a late summer wedding. She wore satin slippers to match her gown. Her bouquet was ruby and white roses. Toni's gown was ruby-red chiffon, and she wore high-heeled satin slippers to match.

Peter was resplendent in a white tuxedo with tails, the bow tie and cummerbund a ruby color to match his bride's dress accents. He had given himself wholly over to her, and she was pleased that he hadn't balked at wearing a color other than black or dark blue to their wedding. His dress shoes were a brilliant white to match his suit. His best man matched him in style and elegance, and both men stood proudly next to the women they squired for the pictures afterwards. They had chosen to be married in Brummen at the Kasteel Engelenburg, and the reception was scheduled for a part of the grounds where they would have a degree of privacy and could dance until their feet fell off.

Though the party was small, the elegance more than made up for any lack of numbers. They took copious amounts of photographs in the beautiful grounds, and there was much laughter during the speeches and toasts. Karen watched Peter's face warm when Jannie, asked to share a memory of her cousin, told of the first time she met Karen months earlier. She described him as "swept away on a tide of feeling" that she had only been praying for four years. She noted that he had probably thought he was hiding the fact that he was smitten from her and Duncan, but that he seemed to have forgotten that they had spent a lot of time together, and she knew him too well to be fooled. George spoke of his devotion to his "baby sister," and of his happiness that at last she had found someone worthy of the generous heart she had.

The reception went on for hours, it seemed, but Peter and Karen slipped away before the end, having done their duty as hosts. Instead of throwing her bouquet, Karen had hugged her friend and handed Toni the bouquet with a sly wink at Niall. Peter surprised Niall by handing him Karen's garter and instructing him to put it to good use. Karen laughed delightedly to see Niall, the confident man she knew, at a loss for words. He reached down to kiss Toni's cheek, and they all cheered. Perhaps there would be another wedding soon.

They had booked the hotel for two nights, and Toni had been charged with wrapping up the festivities. Karen smiled when she returned to their suite and found a bath running, champagne and two glasses already on the side, toiletries and towels ready for their use. She poured in some liquid from a pretty bottle on the side and watched the bubbles rise.

"It would be a shame to spoil this lovely dress by getting it all wet, baby," Peter said in her ear, coming up soundlessly behind her. "Let me help you with it."

She shivered, feeling for all the world like a virginal bride, instead of the woman who had shared his bed for the past two months.

"You are beautiful, sweetie, and you were exquisitely so today." He kissed her tenderly along the line of her neck and went on to kiss her in the hollow of her throat, forgetting for the moment his self-imposed task. His hands wandered over her body in the dress before he wrapped his arms around her and kissed her deeply.

"I love you, *Mevrouw van der Meulen*," he whispered, dropping a light peck on her lips before turning her around to unzip the dress. "Step out of it," he ordered her and held it until she had complied. He draped it over the back of a chair and returned to finish undressing her. When she was naked before him, he kissed her again and moaned when she ran her hand down the hard evidence of his passion for her.

"I love you, too, *Mijnheer van der Meulen*," she said and removed his suit jacket and cummerbund. Untying the bow tie, she used the two ends to pull him to her mouth and laid butterfly kisses on his cheeks, his chin, the strong column of his throat, everywhere but his lips, until he stilled her by grasping her head in his hands and bringing his mouth to hers.

"Tease!" he scolded her but let her finish undressing him.

They stepped into the tub together and sank beneath the frothy bubbles. The water was warm, and they relaxed, stretching their tired limbs before Peter pulled her over to straddle him. He caressed her back, kneading her shoulders gently, then sliding his hands around to treat her breasts to the same tender attention.

"I want you so badly, *liefje*," he confessed, "that I'm not sure I can wait too much longer." He kissed her and thrust his hips up to pierce her waiting warmth. Then he withdrew and reached for the champagne. "Let's drink to our life together, petal," he invited her, and they clinked their glasses and drank deeply. Taking the glass away from her, he said, "Now let's make love."

His last words were muffled by his mouth taking hers, and Karen let herself be swept away by the passion that erupted in her husband. When he had made her come twice and followed her into a third orgasm, he stood with her, unplugged the bath, and rinsed her off with the rain showerhead. Then he dried her and patted her bottom.

"I'll be with you in a moment. I bought you something that I'd like you to wear tonight. It's on the bed."

Karen stepped into the bedroom and saw with some astonishment that a deep ruby red negligee had been set out on the bed. She had an idea of who had helped Peter with this purchase because she recognized it as one she had liked when she and Toni had been shopping for honeymoon nightwear. She remembered Toni distracting her from it, but because she had been happy with what she had chosen, she let it pass. She smiled as she put on the barely-there bikini panties and slid the wispy top over her head. The cut of the front left little to the imagination and was so flimsy she knew if Peter got even a little rough with her, the garment would be irreparably damaged. Her blood pressure rose at the thought.

When he came out of the bathroom, he was wearing a robe that covered all the bits she most wanted to play with. She pouted at him.

"No fair," she said. "I'm all exposed, and you're all hidden."

"Then undress me again, baby," he invited her, a twinkle in his eyes.

The foreplay lengthened between them from the moment she pulled the robe off his shoulders to the second before he plunged into her, taking her body and soul. They made love twice more that night, and Peter wrung cries of bliss from her before finally, exhausted and hoarse, she collapsed against his chest and fell asleep. They didn't manage to wake in time to have breakfast with their guests, who were all waiting indulgently for them to appear. Karen fought against blushing, especially when she remembered their last session in the shower. If she had ever thought older men took longer to get it up, Peter was proving her wrong.

After a pleasant day at the open-air museum in Arnhem, their guests departed, all except for the English ones who would travel with them to Schiphol Airport the next day. Karen spent a few moments with Toni before bed.

"I've never seen you look so radiant, Karen," Toni declared, hugging her tightly. "It's been such a lovely two days with you and Peter. And I'm so pleased to see you so happy!"

"I guess it was just time, eh?" Karen said, smiling. "And if I'm not much mistaken, your time is coming soon."

Toni blushed, surprising Karen. "Well, I don't know about soon, but Niall is a great guy. Thanks for introducing him to me."

"Any time, sweetie! Now, about my fee ..."

Both women burst out laughing, causing heads to turn in their direction.

"I'd better get up to bed. Tomorrow will be a long day." Karen kissed her friend's cheek and said her goodnights, escaping to the calm of her suite. Peter wasn't far behind. By mutual consent, they showered, put on night clothes, and snuggled together.

"*Welterusten, liefje,*" Peter whispered in her ear. "Sleep sweet." He hugged her to his chest and dropped a kiss on the top of her head.

"Night," she answered sleepily, yawning. She didn't know when she fell asleep.

After a day of traveling, Peter took her home to Jamaica. Karen was flabbergasted. She hadn't known his plan, and when he confessed that there would be another Caribbean trip to the two other islands she had told him of at Christmas to finish their honeymoon, her cup of gratitude overflowed.

"Oh Peter, you shouldn't have," she had exclaimed in the airport when she found out where they were going. He had merely smiled at her and hugged her to him.

Now, in the cool of their honeymoon suite, he told her again, "*Ik hou van je, liefje,*" kissing her mouth to the sound of the waves filtering in through the open windows. "I will do everything I can to make you happy."

"You already make me happy, love," she said, letting him pull her with him onto the bed. And that's how they fell asleep, wrapped in each other's arms.

COMING NEXT...

Serendipity 2: Back to Love

Toni and Niall must both make their way back to the love they found when they first met after he discovers who she was previously married to, and she discovers what he does for a living, and it breaks them apart.

Serendipity 3: Back to Last

Chrissy and Rory must decide whether or not they can handle the on-again, off-again affair they have been having since her thirtieth birthday party where they met. Can the feelings they clearly have for each other finally outlast Rory's fear of commitment?

ABOUT THE AUTHOR

KT Bond is an emerging author of contemporary romance across many sub-genres. She started her second career as a ghostwriter of sweet and erotic romances upon her retirement from public education six years ago, giving her clients the love stories that they wanted. Now she writes stories for her own readers, using that experience to show her the way forward. She knows that every life is a tale waiting to be told, and it is her honor and privilege to share the joy of love with you, one story at a time.

KT is a retired English teacher, an avid reader, Nana to an almost four-year-old, and the chief cook and dog walker in her family. She is a member of the Romance Writers of America. This is KT's first book in her own name.

SOCIAL MEDIA

https://linktr.ee/kdjb

4 Horsemen Publications

Romance

Ann Shepphird
The War Council

Emily Bunney
All or Nothing
All the Way
All Night Long: Novella
All She Needs
Having it All
All at Once
All Together
All for Her

Lynn Chantale
The Baker's Touch
Blind Secrets
Broken Lens

Mimi Francis
Private Lives
Private Protection
Run Away Home
The Professor

4HorsemenPublications.com